SARAH'S OWN WAR

SARAH'S OWN WAR

ANNE L. MacDONELL

First published 2023 by Battlebridge Press (Ireland) Ltd

Cataloguing in Publication Data is available from the British Library

ISBN: 978-1-7399171-2-8

Typeset in Palatino 11/15pt

Structural & Developmental Editor: Brian Connolly, Roscommon, Ireland
Production: Mary Gallagher, Roscommon, Ireland
Production consultant: Nicola Kearns, leitrimwritingcottage.com
Typesetting: Paula Elmore, County Westmeath, Ireland

www.battlebridgepress.com

About the Author

ANNE L. MACDONELL lives in the northwest of Ireland now, but is a native of Fort William, Lochaber in the Scottish Highlands. Anne graduated in the Social Sciences and had a career for many years as a Probation Officer in Greater London. This work gave her a great insight into the different ways people cope with life's challenges.

She is a multi-award winning short story writer. Anne's first novel, *Glen Rowan*, was published in 2021. Her novels are inspired by family stories passed down through the generations as she often wondered how her own ancestors had lived and survived throughout the ages, but especially during the eighteenth century, the time of Bonnie Prince Charlie and the Jacobite Rebellion.

ACKNOWLEDGMENTS

I WISH TO EXPRESS MY HEARTFELT gratitude to Mary Gallagher Roscommon Ireland, who played a major role in getting my work developed and completed, and to all the people who got involved in the manuscript and gave constructive feedback, sometimes negative, sometimes positive, but all genuine in their efforts to help me in their own way to construct this novel, which I hope you enjoy. With special thanks also to Renata Lange, Roscommon, Ireland.

CHAPTER 1
1745

'JIMMY! JIMMY! COME back here at once!' Sarah yelled. 'Quick! Quick! Somebody catch him!'

The peat cutting stopped as all the Glen Rowan families turned to look at young James scampering along. As she rushed to stop the boy, Sarah shouted again to the others, 'Don't let him fall in!'

The family knew well the hazards Wee Jimmy was facing. The nearest stopped what they were doing and ran to get closer. Ian Og was the first to get to the boy, grabbing one arm and pulling him away from the vertical edge of the peat bank. Sarah rushed from the other direction. She grasped Wee Jimmy's free arm and Ian Og, thinking his job was done, let go, but Wee Jimmy kept wriggling, trying to free himself, pushing and laughing at Sarah. The bank crumbled. Sarah lost her balance and fell backwards with a splash into a black bog pool. She managed to hold the boy aloft until Ian Og got a firm hold of him again. Young Jimmy had a few splashes of muck on him, but Sarah was soaked from head to toe in the wet black sludge.

It was during this commotion that Uncle Ranald spotted a visitor.

'Well, well, well,' he said. 'Look who it is.' He waved his peat cutter down the glen and everyone turned to watch the lone horseman picking his way up the track.

'It's Alistair!' cried Ian Og, smiling broadly. 'Up here!' he shouted, running towards him.

Although Alistair MacDonell at twenty-three years of age was seven years older than Ian Og, the two were close friends. Together they went hunting wild cats on the hill and, if time allowed, went further afield to look for wolves or catch black grouse in the next glen. They argued, laughed, talked, sang and, over the past five years, had forged a strong bond.

'Have you come to help? Did you bring a spade or a sleàn?' Ian Og shouted eagerly.

Alistair jumped down to hug his young friend. 'I haven't brought a spade or a turf cutter, but nevertheless I think Angus Sticks will be delighted with my cargo.' He nodded towards the sacks strung behind him. 'Is he here? I also have some exciting news.'

'Yes, he is. He said you might be up with some grain in time to celebrate the birthday.'

'Oh dear, I forgot the birthday.' Alistair began to rummage in his sporran and looked up when he heard Sarah's voice.

'Good to see you again, Alistair. You're very welcome, and just in time for some ale and Grannie's herb tea to celebrate the birthday boy.'

'Oh Lord,' he said, as he eyed her up and down. 'Playing in the bog again?'

It was five years since Mammy had died giving birth to Wee Jimmy. Without his dear wife Mary, Dadda had withdrawn into alcohol, leaving his brothers Roderick and 'gentle' Ranald, and brother-in-law Angus to take care of the croft in Glen Rowan. Sarah, then thirteen, being the oldest child, took over her mother's tasks. Over the years and with help from all, young and old, she became 'The Mammy,' earning respect from adults and children alike.

The mucky vision that was Sarah stood before Alistair, beaming.

'Yes. But it was Wee Jimmy who was playing. Ian Og pulled us out.'

Alistair, a favoured nephew of Keppoch, the MacDonell clan chieftain, was a regular visitor to Glen Rowan; he had come nearly every month since Mamma's death and Wee Jimmy's birth. Sarah knew that she wasn't the only one who looked forward to his visits, and she always tried to remind herself that he didn't come especially to see her. The whole family welcomed him and the treats he brought: bannocks to add to the menu and even sweet cake, which was very rare in the glen. A couple of times he'd also brought potatoes and carrots and showed how they were to be planted. They seemed a bit strange at first, but the harvest was stored in the byre and helped to keep them fed over the winter when little else was available.

Alistair smiled and continued searching in his sporran. 'I hope I've something here for the wee man.' He pulled out a delicately laced handkerchief.

Ian Og laughed. 'Where did you get that? One of your many lady friends, I expect. I don't think it'll do for the birthday boy. After all, Wee Jimmy is only five. What else have you got in there?'

Alistair handed the handkerchief to Sarah. 'It's something to wipe your face.' As he continued to scrabble in his sporran, he mumbled, 'Five years? Goodness, the time has gone so quickly. Aha! I have it.' He brought out a small brown nut-shaped lump of tobacco.

Ian Og laughed again. 'Well ... you can tell him it's a manly thing, and he'll have to wait before Dadda says he can use it.' A thought struck him and he stopped abruptly. 'Wait a minute! You didn't come up the glen just for the grain or the birthday. What's going on? What's the news?'

'Yes, you're right' said Alistair. 'I have some news.' He took a deep breath, turned towards everyone working at the peat and raised his voice. 'The young prince, Charles Edward Stuart, has landed, and there's word that the French are behind him, bringing a great army to Ardnamurchan.'

There was a loud cheer from everyone. Spades and sleàns were thrown down and work abandoned. With the news of the prince's landing, everything would change: for Sarah, the family, the glen, the whole countryside. The arrival of Charles, the rightful heir to the throne of Scotland, was a source of great hope and excitement.

When they reached the croft, Roderick and 'gentle' Ranald told Dadda the news and the three immediately fell on their knees to thank God for the saviour sent to deliver them from the Hanoverians. With a loyal toast they drank to the prince. Dadda swore he would not drink whisky again until the usurpers were cast down from the throne, and the rightful heir, Prince Charles, son of James, was crowned King of Scotland. Sarah strongly doubted Dadda's abstinence ability, and immediately stopped the three from smashing the bowls down onto the hearth in their fervour.

As the grown-ups chattered, Wee Jimmy, the birthday boy, kept looking and sniffing at the wee brown knob of tobacco in his hand. He'd promised Alistair that he would keep it safe until Dadda said he was grown up enough to use it, but perhaps a wee nibble now might be a good idea when nobody was watching?

Meanwhile, Grannie Morag organised the children to gather food and drink for everyone. Sarah was at last able to leave the company and get down to the stream where she rinsed the peat muck off herself, and the *lèine* (shirt) and hide she was wearing.

Day merged into night with argument and speculation. Eventually it was decided that Uncle Roderick would go down to MacDonald of Glengarry the following morning and find out what was happening there. Ian Og and younger brother Anghie would visit cousins in Glen Spean and learn their news.

It was nearly dawn when the children finally settled down to sleep and the company took their leave. Sarah went to check on Alistair in the byre. She found him brushing down his faithful horse. He stopped and from one of the saddle packs took out a wee bundle of paper sheets for her, as he had been doing for the past five years.

Sarah had looked after Hamish MacNeil, a young blacksmith's apprentice in Maryburgh, when he'd been badly injured by a soldier five years earlier. In return for her kindness, he had offered to teach her to read and write. Unfortunately, Hamish's earnest efforts did not encourage enthusiastic scholarship, until one day when Alistair was visiting he noted how reluctant a pupil Sarah had become and began to cheer up the lessons with a bit of humour.

To encourage her further, Alistair said that if she learned how to read he would write to her and look forward to receiving replies. True to his word, he wrote letters from time to time, sending them with any passing traveller. At first the words were very simple, and it took a while before she could read them all by herself. Paper was a rare commodity in the glen, and Alistair began to send bits of paper, most of it already used, which he had collected during his travels: thick, thin, dark, white, smooth or creased but always with one side clear. Sarah kept the scraps carefully in the precious carved wooden box that had always held Mamma's mementos. It took time and effort for her to decipher what was written: notes, curt instructions, household lists. In time when she felt more confident, she would take a slip of paper and on the unwritten side carefully practise her writing.

With Ian Og's reluctant encouragement and using the family bible, Sarah learned to read and write quite well, but it was nearly a year before she found enough courage to write a short letter to Alistair, using one of the scarce sheets of paper. She sent the note with Uncle Angus, who was returning to Strontian and would eventually meet Alistair in Maryburgh, the little town beside Fort William. It was brief.

'Aliztr I am wel. Thank you for the papr.'

It opened a window for her into the vast world beyond the glen.

Sometimes life was hard and food scarce, but the whole family in Glen Rowan was kind and caring. Grannie Morag was rather vague at times, but still kept everyone in check while they shared the good and the bad. Alistair's visits were always welcome, especially to Sarah. He brought more to her than sheets of paper or food treats, and although the attention he paid to her seemed no greater than what he gave to the others, he always made her feel special.

'You'll be off soon,' she said. 'I'll go and get some food for your journey.'

Alistair patted the horse and settled himself on the ground beside his saddle.

'Don't rush away,' he said. 'Please ... come ... Sit here beside me for a moment. It's been a long day and night, and I haven't heard any of your own news. It is always good to get your wee notes and Ian Og says you are still working hard on the Scots reading and writing.'

'Oh yes.' Wearily, Sarah sat down. 'He has been quite strict. Often calls me when I am busy with other things. But he means well and helps with the young ones.'

'You are very kind to them all,' said Alistair, gently taking her hand in his.

She didn't take hers away.

'They're all very good really. Grannie is still a great help although her mind wanders more and more.'

His touch was more than comforting in its warmth, and when he moved closer, she didn't pull away either.

The gentle nuzzle into her neck gave her a rare spark of comfort, and she sighed softly with pleasure. Slowly it became a kiss on her neck and she sighed again, her neck slowly stretching to accept the next kiss, and almost of its own accord, her head turned to let her lips feel the magic for themselves. It was several minutes before she pushed him away.

'Oh Alistair, we can't do this, not now ... not yet.'

Reluctantly, Alistair stood up.

'You're right. I have stayed much longer than I should.' He lifted the saddle and strapped it onto his horse. 'The prince's business cannot be delayed.' He bent down for a final kiss. 'I must go now. As soon as I return, I will talk to your Dadda.'

He led the animal out of the byre, mounted and, with a final wave, kicked it into a lively trot. All too soon, he was out of sight.

Although disappointed that Alistair had left so suddenly, Sarah tingled with elation, so she closed her eyes to relive their kiss. His words – 'I will talk to your Dadda' – echoed over and over in her head. Filled with excitement and walking on air, she returned to the house. Everyone was asleep, and she sat by herself, savouring what had just happened.

Early next day, Uncle Roderick rode off to Keppoch Castle at Invergarry for news, returning speedily in the afternoon, bringing word that the men should prepare to move. They were to gather four days hence. Anticipation coloured the atmosphere like peat smoke on a still day, and word spread like wildfire. The garrisons at Fort William, Fort Augustus and up at Ruthven were on full alert already. In the glen, men would absent themselves, later returning with flintlock pistols, muskets and even old firelocks, smeared in rancid sheep lard and wrapped in old hide. Dadda and Uncle Roderick came home with broadswords one day, and on the next unearthed small, round, leather-backed shields from under the peat stack.

Claymores and swords were cleaned and sharpened. The rhythmic slither of metal on whetstone became a constant melody in the glen, and tension began to mount. The women helped out as well. Wee Morag was put to work on the spinning wheel, and Eileen was set to knitting stockings to help clothe the fighting men. *Lèintean* were stitched, plaids and bonnets washed and mended. Grannie Morag could no longer be trusted to make up her medicines, but she kept the soup pot bubbling with every spare scrap of food, and saw that all were fed.

Sarah now had the task of making healing ointments from goose grease and sheep fat, with knitbone and selfheal, willow bark, meadowsweet and other herbs from Grannie's precious store. She made up a little package for each man, reminding him of the uses for every herb. She wished she was going with them, but her duty was with Grannie and the young ones.

Patriotic fervour infected everyone. Old ones gave the younger ones unheeded advice, and sat by the fire each night telling heroic stories to the whirring of the spinning wheel. 'Those were the days.' Pipes were puffed contentedly. 'A man could profit well in a cattle raid.' Heads nodded sagely. 'And marry on the proceeds.'

Old arguments were reprised. The story of Ian the Limp was legendary. He was injured in a fight with Crow Nose Duncan, during a dispute which had taken place over twenty years ago. It left him with a broken leg that never fully healed, and ever since he was known as Ian the Limp. Few could remember what the dispute was about.

'The chief's word was law then.' The old folk nodded and mused together. 'There was respect for the elders too.' The nods became sorrowful shakings. 'Not like nowadays, children arguing and talking back.' Indrawn breath through missing teeth and an occasional 'tsk tsk' confirmed the decline of the young people in the glen.

'Maybe this fight will put fire into their bellies, and teach them what life is really about.' Pipes and mugs were refilled and more old stories were retold. Infernos already raged within the bellies of their offspring. While the ancients bemoaned the passing of olden days, the clan youth anticipated victory and glory. They wanted to impress their peers, and maybe catch the attention of one or two of the maids, who – purely by chance, of course – regularly passed the field where they played a bit of shinty, or kicked a bladder about. Now they spent their time in that field mock-fighting and wrestling in preparation for the anticipated battles ahead.

Ian Og was also full of fire. The past five years had seen him fill out. Not yet as tall as his father, the strong lean adult shape was there, and he was itching to prove he could fight with the best of them. In his head he planned exploits in which he rescued the beleaguered prince from danger, and became his henchman, the principal attendant of the most principal of Highland chiefs, standing always at his shoulder. Unfortunately, he did not have a sword. A couple of lads in the glen who did were the envy of the rest. The smith was busy, day and night, making and mending weapons for the men, and pouring metal into moulds for shot. Youth would have to wait its turn. They met in quiet places to practise with sticks and clubs. Ian Og's speciality, the sling shot, although deadly, was a poor substitute for cold steel.

One morning as he was practising at home, trying to knock a tin cup off some stones, Grannie Morag called him. 'Come,' she commanded, crooking her finger so that he would follow.

'I can't just now, Grannie. I have to practise.'

She grasped his wrist with bony fingers and pulled him with her. 'Never mind that,' she said. Out of the house they went, determined woman and reluctant youth.

'But Grannie,' he protested wearily. 'Where are you taking me?'

'Always questions!' She shook her head, and as they passed the byre she pointed to a spade. 'Pick that up.' Despite her failing intellect, she seemed to know well enough not to let go of his wrist. Then she pulled him out towards the old graveyard. Ian Og was beginning to get uneasy.

For months, Grannie Morag had been growing increasingly strange. She was losing touch with everyone around her, sometimes mistaking them for people long dead, and getting angry when the pattern of her life didn't make sense to her. Sometimes she would call down curses upon everything around her, with a vitriolic vehemence that shocked them all at first, but even the young ones were becoming used to it. They had learned that holding and gently stroking Grannie's hand soon brought her back to a semblance of her old self.

So it was with some concern that Ian Og viewed the little graveyard. It was just a walled enclosure with five slightly raised overgrown areas in it, but he was afraid of what the demented old lady wanted him to do. Granddad wasn't buried here, having died in 1715 at Sherrifmuir, but the loose cairn of stones that was his memorial made a sixth mound. Grannie usually added a stone every time she came, but this time she turned to Ian Og.

'Now dig,' she said, as though this were the obvious course of action.

'What? The cairn?' asked Ian Og. He didn't like where this was going.

'Yes.' The rebuke in her tone suggested she thought he was simple-minded. 'Yes, dig Granddad's cairn.' She tapped it with her foot. Ian Og felt a mild horror. Even though the bones of his Granddad were not buried here, the cairn was treated as though they were.

'Oh no, Grannie,' he protested.

'Oh yes, Ian Og,' she countered. 'Do you think I'm mad?' she added, challenging him to speak his mind. He could not meet her direct gaze, her age-dulled eyes suddenly sparking with their old fire. 'Well, are you going to start, or am I going to have to do it myself?' She bent down and started to pull stones away from the plot.

'No … No, Grannie,' said Ian Og. It was wrong to disturb the mound, but it would be a greater wrong to let Grannie injure herself. Hastily he began to help her, as he tried to think of a way to stop without offending the mindless old woman.

'Get the spade. It's not very deep,' she said.

'What isn't?' Ian Og asked.

'You'll see, boy. Come on.' She was impatient so Ian Og decided it best to humour her and he began to dig in earnest. The spade struck something.

'There it is!' she squeaked with delight. 'Be careful now.'

The two of them bent down to retrieve a long hidebound packet, to which the dank earth clung stubbornly. The shape was unmistakable.

'Grannie … It's a sword!'

The old woman began to unwrap it. 'Aye, it was Granddad's. He took his best to Sherrifmuir and left this one here in case we needed it. I buried it when he didn't come back.'

She handed the soggy lump to the young man. 'I don't know how well it will have lasted. I coated it in fir resin, which should have protected it, but thirty years is a long time. If it is still any good, I know he would be proud for you to use it.'

Ian Og unwound the deerskin wrapping and lifted his grandfather's sword, a fire burning in his belly.

'Thank you, Grannie, and thank you, Granddad,' he said with pride. 'It still looks good. A bit pitted here and there, but it seems sound.' He threw his arms around Grannie and kissed her. Thinking about that day later, Ian Og would realise it was the last meaningful conversation he had with Grannie Morag.

On returning to the croft, Ian Og's new possession drew attention.

'That's our Dadda's sword!' Uncle Ranald exclaimed when he saw Ian Og's prize. At first Dadda and Uncle Roderick couldn't believe it, but upon examination agreed the weapon was indeed their own father's sword.

'No better man to bear it,' said Roderick. 'But it needs a lot work on it. Get to the burn and rub sand into it to remove the coating and the rust, and then we'll find you a good stone to shine it up and start giving it an edge. It's likely we will be leaving soon, and you'll need it.'

CHAPTER 2

Grannie Morag, Sarah, Anghie and the younger children stood together as they waved the proud men down the track, their plaids neat and each bonnet jaunty and trimmed with a generous clump of heather, the badge of the clan. Once they were gone, stillness hung over the glen. Not even the birds had the heart to sing.

It didn't take long for the Glen Rowan men to reach the MacDonell chief's home, Keppoch Castle, overlooking Glen Spean and Glen Roy. Ian Og was expecting to see a crowd drawn up and ready to march off to war, but there were only a handful of men standing or sitting under a couple of trees. When they were close enough they saw none were strangers.

'Just in time,' Big John called to them.

As they joined the men in the courtyard, Roderick went into the castle to hear the discussion that was taking place about the best use of the men while they waited for orders. Outside, under the trees, the men speculated about how soon they would be marching south. There was no question that they would drive the usurper Hanoverians from the thrones of Scotland and England. There was also talk that the French army was soon to land at Ardnamurchan, and join them.

'Aye, those milksop southerners won't know what's hit them. We've let them rule the roost for far too long.'

'Still, it'll be a hard fight.'

'No! Once they see we have the rightful king's son with us, they'll flock to the cause.'

'You could be right. I have a cousin in Edinburgh and she says that the people are sick of them taking everything away from Scotland and giving us nothing. The taxes are terrible.'

'They can't take much from us. We have little enough to keep the family fed.'

'But they do it anyway. Take the gaugers.'

'The gaugers?'

'Yes, the gaugers. That's the London government for you. They send men up to the hills to stop the whisky.'

'Well, they haven't stopped it yet.'

'Not here. But out beyond the hills.' The speaker paused. 'They know where nearly every still is. Then they tax it.'

'That's like taxing air.'

'That's governments.' It was said with the finality of a clinching argument.

Movement from the house stopped the discussion and Roderick returned. 'We have to guard the road. Keep an eye on comings and goings.'

'Where are we going to guard?'

'Some are heading for the new High Bridge and others to the Braes. We'll head for Gairlochy and maybe link up with the Achnacarry men. Get more news there.'

'This is more like it,' thought Ian Og as he strode along at the back of the group. He was ready for anything. His sword hung from his belt, bright now from sanding and polishing, and with an edge his Granddad would have been proud of. It could cut in half any man unlucky enough to stand in his way. All he wanted to make his life complete was a firearm. Dadda and Uncle Roderick gave him some practice with theirs. It was a bit tricky to judge the time delay between the flint spark and ignition, but now he could nearly always hit whatever he aimed at unless it was too far away.

It was late afternoon when they reached the river at Gairlochy. They'd taken their time on the road, and were wary that there might be government spies among the other travellers. On the road, they'd met some who were hastening away from Fort William, expecting an attack at any moment. Many were heading the other way, hoping to find refuge there whenever hostilities began. A herd of cattle, too, was making steady progress towards Loch Treig. It would cross the River Spean on the old track, the drovers hoping to avoid the attention of any belligerents and get well beyond the Highland line before the insurrection began. A herd of cattle would fill plenty of fighting bellies, and the drovers would be the losers. The Glen Rowan men were not out for beef this day and paid no heed to the animals, only nodding to the drovers, who held charged muskets at the ready, cautiously keeping their distance from the clansmen.

At Gairlochy, where the loch slowly drained into the river, the ground was marshy and offered little cover, so they settled themselves to wait on the nearby hillside, behind rocks and under heather clumps. The worst of having to wait in one place were the clegs: flies that live on deer and horses and like to taste the flesh of man. Most of the older men were unaffected by the bites, hardly bothering to slap or squash the predators, but Ian Og found them quite a trial. When Dadda saw how much they liked him, he pointed to a bushy clump of elder a hundred yards along the valley. 'Go and get yourself some of that elder. Rub yourself down. It'll stop the itch for a while. If you had a pipe, I'd give you a fill of tobacco.'

As he didn't have a pipe, Ian Og quietly made his way towards the tree and began to pull off some leaves and rub them onto his skin. He wore rough hide footwear, a *lèine* and his plaid, so he sat down to apply the leaves more easily to his bare legs and buttocks. After a minute or two, he heard a sound: a throat being cleared. Someone was moving quietly along the riverside. Ian Og shuffled himself further into the cover of the bushy leaves, half-afraid the beating of his heart would be heard.

'*This should be a good place to wait,*' a voice in Scots whispered. '*Those heathens will be passing all the time. We'll learn all we need to know by morning.*' He slapped himself. '*These damned midges!*'

'*Be still,*' hissed his companion. '*And don't blaspheme! And don't light up that pipe or we'll have every clansman for miles down on us. They can track a fish in water, some of 'em, so don't give 'em any help.*'

The two settled in the shelter of the elder bush behind two boulders. They would have a grandstand view of the goings-on at Gairlochy, which was an important crossroad linking MacDonald and Cameron lands. They were too close for Ian Og to move away without being seen, and he knew he had no chance of tackling two spying soldiers on his own.

It was a blessing that at least the clegs were keeping away, while he pondered what to do. Staying out of sight, he picked up several large pebbles. Using his sling he lobbed one as far as he could towards the clansmen. It made a click as it hit a rock and Ian Og hoped one of his kin could hear it.

'*What was that?*' said one of the soldiers.

The next couple of stones must have landed on vegetation because there was no sound. Then 'click' again.

'*Someone's there.*'

'*Stay quiet. It's quite far away. If we sit tight they won't know we're here.*'

As they spoke there was another 'click'.

'*I tell you there's someone there.*'

'*Be quiet! Look! There's no one there.*'

It was the next 'click' that roused the soldiers into retreat.

'*God, I don't like this. We'd better move.*'

'*Do NOT take the name of the Lord in vain!*'

The two began to crawl out of their hiding place and were immediately confronted by Uncle Roderick and Big John, who stood, swords drawn, with a look of steely determination on their faces. Their swords flashed in unison and with a soft *whump*, the two soldiers fell lifeless into the heather.

Ian Og was stunned. Uncle Roderick grasped a handful of vegetation and drew it along his sword to clean it, before he came and patted him on the shoulder. 'Well done, Ian Og.' He looked down on the two bodies. 'There'll be a lot more of that before we're done. That's what we're here to do. Stop information getting back to the fort.'

'What'll we do with these now?' asked Ian Og.

'They may as well go under the bush. They'll miss them eventually at the fort, but we needn't make a present of them until they smell. We'll take anything useful.'

Big John began to rummage at the man he had just killed. 'These shoes will fit someone. Look and see what else they've got. Usually they have bread or biscuits too.'

'Can I have one of the pistols?' Ian Og asked.

'Help yourself. You'll certainly need one and you've earned it. Don't forget the shot and powder.'

As he delved into the man's pockets, Ian Og found a pipe and tobacco pouch. He took that as well before the gory cargo was dumped unceremoniously under the shelter of the bush. They re-joined the others on watch. Everyone was now even more alert.

When Ian Og sat himself down to rest against a fir tree, he laid his new treasures on his lap to inspect them, but soon he fell asleep.

'It's time to move.' Uncle Ranald's words woke him up, about an hour later. 'Lochiel's men are taking over here and we're moving up the Lochy.'

Ian Og knew some of their replacements, Donald Cameron and his brother Kenneth, and acknowledged them with a sideways tilt of his head.

'We heard you got two soldiers last night,' said Donald.

'Well, I didn't actually kill them.' He spoke modestly. 'I spotted them and set them up for the others. Look. I got one of the pistols.'

The young men admiringly handled the weapon.

'That's a good weight and whatever else you might say about the soldiers, they know how to look after their weapons.'

It was with a little reluctance that Ian Og left the scene of his triumph and his two friends and admirers, but duty called. As he trailed behind the others, he found a long thin reed, which he used to clear out the stem of the confiscated pipe. The tarry outside he cleaned by scraping it with the edge of his knife, and by the time they reached their station on the slopes by Loch Lochy, Ian Og considered that almost every trace of the previous owner had been removed. He filled it from his newly acquired pouch and begged a spark of light from his father.

There were some broad smiles from his kin as he drew earnestly at the pipe to get the tobacco properly lit, but it wasn't long before he had a satisfactory glow in the bowl, and puffs of rich smoke emerged from the side of his mouth. It appeared that Ian Og was no stranger to a pipe and tobacco. When Dadda and the uncles realised that he would not be making a fool of himself, they turned to other things and settled to keep watch. Ian Og, with sword, pistol and pipe, sat down and took his place among the men.

CHAPTER 3

TEN DAYS LATER, IAN Og proudly strode down the hillside with the rest of the Glen Rowan MacDonells into Glenfinnan. Spread out before them on the plain at the head of Loch Shiel was a large assembly of highlanders. He had never seen so many people in one place before.

Sometimes in the summer, when men boasted about their strength, or their skill with the caman, the local clans would meet and hold trials of wrestling or of throwing a large stone. Sometimes they played riotous games of shinty, in which everyone would take part. There was always music too, for dancing, singing and courting. These gatherings brought people together from several glens, and maybe filled a field to overflowing, but this was much bigger.

'We'll surely beat the Hanoverians with all these men, Dadda. There must be hundreds and hundreds,' said Ian Og.

His father shook his head. 'We'll need more than

this. You should have seen us during the "Fifteen" rebellion.' A faraway look of pride came over the older man's face. 'We were a mighty host then, but it wasn't the right time. That was a long time ago. This is the right time now.' He pulled himself up to his full proud stocky height. 'We'll beat them because our cause is just, and we have the rightful king's son to lead us.'

'He'll be here, won't he?' Ian Og was looking forward to seeing the much-heralded prince who would lead them to righteous victory.

'Of course he will. Look down there. See that tent – over there on that wee bit of high ground? There's a foreign-looking group of strangers. One of those men is the prince.'

Ian Og squinted hard, but although he could see the a big white tent, it was too far away to distinguish any person of obvious nobility.

By the time they joined the mass of highlanders below, it was afternoon. Ranald of the Rocks marched proudly in front of them. The streamers on his bagpipe drones fluttered in the wind as he piped the last half mile or so, to where they drew up beside other MacDonells. With his work done for the moment, the piper went off to a quiet spot behind some bushes, to wet his whistle with a sup of whisky, and to adjust the reeds of his instrument.

When he was ready and with his back to the crowd, he struck up a stirring tune on the bagpipes, while all waited for history to set its momentous hand upon the gathering. Every now and again the melody would be held on one note as he stood still and adjusted the drones, or took another mouthful from the flask in his sporran. Further along, several other pipers practised, snatches of different tunes floating in the air.

The Glen Rowan clansmen were more interested in what was happening by the tent.

'What are we waiting for?' asked Ian Og eagerly of the other Keppoch men.

'Who knows?' was the bored answer. 'We've been here for an hour or more and we've seen nothing yet, except the prince, of course.'

'You saw the prince?'

'Yes, that's him over there ... by the tent! Can you see?'

Heads turned to look where the grubby finger pointed. They saw a young man in a plain dun-coloured coat, with flashes of red catching the eye when he moved.

'Who are the others?'

'We're not sure. Someone said the one talking to the prince is Gordon of Glenbucket.'

'Is he still alive?' said Dadda, peering at him. 'I thought he was dead.'

'By the creaky look of him, he ought to be.'

'Ah no,' Dadda protested. 'He's a good man and I'm fairly sure that the other crippled one there is one of the Duke of Atholl's family.' Still sober, Dadda was enjoying being the fountain of knowledge for all those around.

'He looks pretty creaky too,' someone commented.

'The prince is young enough anyway,' Ian Og was fascinated by the young man.

'Look, he's talking to some woman now. Would that be his wife?'

'No, not at all.' Dadda was scornful. 'Look at her. She's a Highland woman. I've seen her before. I can't remember her name, though.' He scratched his head. 'I think she is one of the Cameron women from up Glen

Dessary way. She's as old as I am. He could have his pick of all the grand ladies and princesses, so he wouldn't be after some wife from Glen Dessary.' He grinned. 'Mind you, she might do for an old widower like me.'

The others laughed as Ian Og asked again, 'But what are they all waiting for?'

'I think they're waiting for more clansmen to arrive,' said one.

'No,' another voice answered. 'They're waiting for the guns to get here.'

Yes. I heard they're bringing them up the loch from Kinlochmoidart.'

'Are they bringing muskets?' Ian Og asked eagerly. I'd like to have one as well as my pistol.'

'Yes. Muskets, cannons, gunpowder, shot. They'll bring everything!'

More men were approaching and the MacDonells stood aside for them to pass. Locheil's own piper marched ahead of four other pipers, all clad in identical new plaids, with fresh ribbon lacing their drones and fluttering in the breeze. This heralded the arrival of the Cameron men. Locheil, their chieftain, rode at the head of them, the oak badge on his bonnet further embellished with a long eagle feather. Behind were his men marching proudly in step, escorting two lines of red-uniformed Royal Scots soldiers, they had captured. They had ambushed them at the High Bridge two days earlier. It was a fine spectacle.

'Aww, Dadda,' said Ian Og. 'That could have been us, if we'd stayed there instead of going to Gairlochy.'

'Ian Og. You take a look at the Cameron men. They did well with what they had. They captured some passing soldiers, but the two spies we killed would have caused more damage than all of them.'

Looking again at the Camerons more carefully, Ian Og turned to his father. 'Most of them have no weapons at all.'

'Aye, we can let them have their glory. They'll need it. And some weapons,' he added.

For Ian Og, however, there was a more pressing need. 'What about something to eat?' he asked. 'I'm hungry.'

'You'll have to wait,' was the unhelpful reply from another. 'The food is coming with the weapons, but there's no sign of any boats yet.'

Ian Og was disappointed. He was used to hunger but he hadn't eaten since the previous morning. He thought there would have been some food when they reached Glenfinnan. 'I'll go and take a look on the hill. Maybe there's something, berries, sorrel, anything.'

'I think there were a few scavenging there already. You'd be as well waiting here.'

It may have been sensible advice, but Ian Og felt sure that even if there was nothing left, he would be able to find some small animal that would succumb to his trusty sling.

As he began to make his way through the groups of highlanders, he noticed one of the prince's entourage passing through the crowd towards him. He wore a blue linen coat and tartan kilt, with a white lacy linen shirt, buckled shoes, and a matching blue hat with a white feather. He was like a butterfly among the muted reds and greens of the plaided highlanders.

'Well, well, laddie? Deserting the prince already?'

He knew it was a familiar voice all right, but it took a moment or two to pick out the features of this elegant courtier. 'Alistair! I didn't recognise you.'

'Yes, I guess the clothes make a difference, don't they?'

Ian Og could only nod.

'But where are you off to?'

'I'm going to look for sorrel or something. We thought the food would be here by now.'

'When did you eat?' said Alistair, fishing within his coat and bringing out half a thick oat bannock which he handed to his cousin.

'Yesterday morning.' The reply was mumbled through the food. When Alistair handed him the other half, Ian Og beamed. 'Thanks. Is it all right if I share it with Dadda and the uncles?'

'You do what you like with it. Where are they? Go and tell them I'll be over in a minute.'

'They won't know you!'

It was about an hour before Alistair, carrying a loose bundle, made it over to the family. There was plenty of teasing about his grand appearance, but he grinned good-naturedly. 'There is meat being cooked now. Look: see that smoke over there. There aren't enough pots to boil it all up, so some of it is just going to be grilled on the fire, but when you're hungry ...'

Dadda turned to Ian Og. 'Get over there, lad.'

'No need.' Alistair drew the family together and triumphantly opened his bundle. Glistening in its folds lay five generous slices of beef charred black by the fire. There were also chunks of bread.

'Oh Alistair,' said Dadda, 'You must have a pact with the devil.'

The men around them were taking notice of the smell.

'Over there,' Alistair pointed to the smoke at the edge of the gathering, and soon they were gone, leaving the family alone.

'How did you manage the meat?' Dadda asked.

'Not me. It was Locheil. When he realised there weren't any food supplies, he got some cattle brought up. I just happened to know about it. And the bread, well … just say it was a donation from the prince himself.'

'Look!' said Ian Og. 'Something's happening.'

Sure enough the people around the prince were starting to arrange themselves in a line facing the highlanders.

'I'd better get back,' said Alistair. 'I wanted to have a word with you, Dadda, but I'm supposed to be Keppoch's aide, so I must go.'

Swiftly he turned and left.

'Can you see what's happening?' Dadda asked.

'No, I can't see very much.' Ian Og sighed.

'I can!' Uncle Roderick was the tallest of the three brothers. 'I can see Bishop Hugh. He's in full vestments. He's blessing something that I can't make out. He's sprinkling holy water on it.' He paused momentarily. 'Oh now I can see it. It's the flag. It's being lifted by your Duke of Atholl, Dadda.'

The others could at last see the top of the flag.

'Hush,' said Ian Og. 'I can nearly make out what he's saying.' But after some moments he had to admit he could hear very little. 'I can't even say what language he's speaking.'

Finally, the prince himself mounted a fine white horse and spoke out to the crowd.

'That's better,' said Dadda. Then he frowned. 'What's he saying?'

Ian Og cocked his ears. 'Em, it's Gaelic. This is a great … something we can tell our grandchildren. More clans … Hanoverian usurpers … country ready… Edinburgh … London … people … together … I think he's stopped. Yes, look. He's lifting the banner.'

The standard began to flap in the wind. The prince raised it aloft with both hands and a loud cheer rose from the crowd. It seemed that the ceremony was over.

'What happens now?' Ian Og asked.

'We wait,' Dadda answered. 'See what the Keppoch clans are doing, and then we'll probably get off home for a couple of days. If they're heading for Edinburgh, they'll likely pass near us.'

'Are we going to get some arms and provisions?' asked Ian Og, adding, 'There are no boats in the loch.'

'Donald Keppoch will tell us all about that, but you get up there and see if there's anything else to be had. We could use some meal.'

'Will we attack the forts?' There was enthusiasm in Ian Og's voice.

Dadda was matter-of-fact. 'That's what they will tell us before we go. They'll need us if they're doing that.'

CHAPTER 4

'WHO IS IT?' THE VOICE pierced the darkness around the croft.

Through the howling of the wind came the crackle of rustling footsteps, and a voice quietly called out, 'It's only me.'

'Ian Og? What are you doing, frightening us to death like that?' Sarah sounded both querulous and relieved. 'I thought it was soldiers. It's been so quiet here since everyone left, but they had soldiers over in Glen Roy a couple of times.' She turned back into the croft. 'Come in and don't make a noise. We don't want to wake Grannie up.'

Instead of following, Ian Og turned away towards the byre, calling back over his shoulder, 'Give us a hand, Sarah. He got shot. I've got to leave him here.'

'Who got shot?' There was alarm in Sarah's voice. 'Who's with you?'

'It's me, Sarah.' A faint voice reached her.

'Who's that?' She held up the lantern and peered

into the darkness, where she could see a man leaning heavily on Ian Og. 'Hamish? It's Hamish! I hardly recognised you. What happened?'

'We were doing a job for Alistair. He went off with the prince.'

They shuffled into the pale light.

'What were you doing?'

Her question was understandable. The vision before her was caked in mud and blood. Even in the poor flickering light of her suet candle, his face was deathly pale. 'Sorry, Sarah. I always seem to be coming to you for assistance.'

'We were heading for Achnacarry,' Ian Og explained. 'Some soldiers ambushed us and Hamish was shot, so I brought him here. I can't stay long.'

'Were you followed?'

'I hope not.' Ian Og half-dragged his companion closer to the light.

'Oh! Dear Lord,' Sarah put her hand to her mouth. 'Look at that leg. And you've walked all the way up here on it.'

'No. We have a garron. Her name is Sneeshan and we took turns with her. I couldn't let Hamish walk so I ran alongside the beast.' Ian Og looked exhausted.

'Well, that's something.'

Sarah came outside to help support Hamish. 'Come on. Let's get him inside, but remember, keep quiet or Grannie will hear us.'

Anghie was already up from his bed in the corner. Like Sarah, he'd heard odd sounds in the night and when he realised who was arriving, he revived the fire and put potatoes into the old iron pot on the embers. The three shuffled awkwardly through the low door and put Hamish onto Dadda's chair.

Sarah kindled a pine stick. It spluttered, and then flared. She drew a deep breath and began to inspect the bloodied leg. Both faces before her were grey and drawn.

'We'll need a good dram, Anghie,' she said, then gingerly began to peel the mash of leaves from Hamish's wound.

'Oh! Yeuch, how did you do this?' she asked as the dark green tatters reluctantly parted from the flesh, and the four of them looked at a ragged hole in Hamish's taut muscled thigh.

While they inspected the damage, Anghie passed a large bowl of whisky to each of them.

'Is the ball out?' Sarah asked.

'No,' said Ian Og. 'We couldn't stop. I just grabbed some leaves and hoped for the best.'

'You did well enough.' Sarah nodded as she sipped her whisky. 'It would probably be much worse if you'd just left it and put nothing around the wound.'

Ian Og drained his bowl and set it down on the table. 'Aahh, that was good!' He laid his hand on Sarah's shoulder, as he turned to the door. 'You'll see to him. I must go. I'll make better time now.'

'Wait a minute.' Anghie pointed to the pot on the fire. 'You'll need something to eat before you go.'

'No, no, Anghie, thanks. I don't think I can wait for potatoes.'

'They're nearly done, or maybe a couple of bannocks then.' He laid several on the table with some cheese. 'What about another wee dram of whisky to see you on your way? It won't delay you more than a minute.'

The temptation was too much for a very tired and hungry young man. It made good sense to refuel before the next part of his journey.

'All right then, a couple of bannocks and a dram.

It could be a while before I get anything more to eat again.'

As he sat again and began to eat, his attention was brought back to the patient by a groan from Hamish, as Sarah probed the wound.

'Lucky it didn't smash the bone,' Sarah commented, fetching her sharp knife from its niche beside the fire and a clean linen rag.

'Lucky it wasn't a funeral,' Hamish jested weakly from between clenched teeth. 'Good job his aim was poor.'

He drained his whisky and nodded assent to Sarah. Swiftly, she probed with the knife through the flesh and scooped around the edge of the mangled lead ball, loosening it for her searching fingers to retrieve triumphantly. All four sighed with relief. None had dared to breathe until the task was completed.

Ever helpful, Anghie was ready with a pitcher of warm salty water, and at Sarah's nod he poured it gently over the wound, making Hamish cry out. Sarah passed the last of her own dram to Hamish and began to clean up the wound.

'What exactly happened?' asked Sarah as she threaded a large needle with a couple of horsehairs and began to stitch the edges of flesh together.

Hamish gulped another mouthful of whisky from the bowl, which Anghie refilled, before answering. 'We were moving quickly, taking a message to the prince at Achnacarry. Someone must have been watching us.' He winced again.

Ian Og came to look at Sarah's handiwork, and took up the story between mouthfuls of bannock.

'It wasn't far from the crossing at Spean near the old track, so we took the Ruthven path to confuse them.'

'You were being followed?' Sarah's eyes opened wide in alarm.

'No.' Ian Og was scornful. 'They just happened to be there spying. They couldn't follow a pregnant cow. We doubled back and took the shortcut over the back of Glen Roy.'

'They're not foolish,' Sarah insisted. 'They won't take long to work out where you went and Glen Roy will be running with soldiers again.'

'No,' said Ian Og again, this time with confidence. 'There was only one or maybe two of them at most, because the rest are back at the fort. They think we're fetching an army.'

'What made them think you were going to get an army?'

Hamish smiled up at her. 'I might have given them that impression.'

The whisky was having an effect on his empty stomach. The pain was easing but he was struggling to stay awake, and as Sarah made the final knot, his head sagged.

Sarah laid willow leaves on the wound and began to bandage it up with a long linen strip. She asked Ian Og as she worked, 'How did he do that ... I mean, make them think you were bringing an army?'

'Well, Hamish was in Maryburgh and deliberately let slip to several people that he heard it would be wise to be elsewhere: his boss, Cameron the smith, Black Duncan the butcher, people like that. It soon got about.'

The clatter of the potato pot lid distracted him for a moment. He resumed the tale. 'People left. Some went into the fort.' He stuck his knife into the pot and sighed appreciatively. 'I could murder a couple of those potatoes, but I've got to get the horse and be on my way.'

As Sarah ripped the last piece of the bandage into two tails to tie around Hamish's leg, she nodded to her younger brother. 'Anghie will get the horse. You rest for a moment and you can take some potatoes with you.'

'Thanks, Anghie. She's down by the burn,' said Ian Og as he lifted the pot from the chain over the fire, and drained the water onto a clump of heather stalks on the earthen floor in the corner.

'I'm starving,' he said as he tipped out the contents of the pot onto the table.

'Me too,' said, Hamish, roused by the enticing smell. The quiet whisper was firmer now as he gingerly reached over and took one of the steaming potatoes.

'Come on then, Ian Og,' said Sarah, 'Tell me. What you have been up to since Glenfinnan? Dadda said you'd gone off with Alistair. I don't suppose he sent me any message?'

'It was great, Sarah.' He bit appreciatively into a potato and spoke through the hot pieces. 'Alistair and I took cannons down to Ardgour. The prince brought them. They were only small and we didn't have a lot of powder or any supplies.' He sprinkled some salt on the potato and took another bite. 'It was hard, even with the horses. But we got them set up at the narrows. Alistair, Donald Maclean from Glen Scaddle and others helped us.' He got more excited as he told of the events. 'There were lots more on the Ardgour side, and Onich and Glencoe men on this side, and the guns pointing down Loch Linnhe to the sea. Well … a couple of guns. But they are expecting more.'

'So you've been manning empty cannons all this time?'

'No,' he mumbled through mouthfuls of potato. 'I

mean, we all helped with the cannons, but my job was to carry messages.'

'What: to Locheil and Keppoch?' asked Sarah as she made sure that Hamish could reach the salt and fetched a pitcher of thick sour milk.

Ian Og took a deep draught before handing it to Hamish. 'Yes. No,' he wiped his mouth. 'It was mostly between Ardgour, Corran and Onich. I had to swim a couple of times too.'

'So, what was happening in Onich?'

'We were there to keep an eye out for government relief boats, and stop them getting up Loch Linnhe. If they couldn't get past us, they'd try somewhere else along the shore.'

'Did they try it?'

'Oh yes. They came up the narrows on the rising tide. But we were waiting. Oh, Sarah, you should have seen it. They thought they were going to get away with it, but we let them have it. Missed on the first ball, but we'd have got them on the second if they hadn't turned away smartly. Even shot at us!' Seeing Sarah's alarmed face, he added, 'But they were nowhere near. We just need some more cannons and cannon balls.'

Sarah refilled the whisky in each bowl, but Hamish's head was already lolling back against the wall and he fell asleep as Ian Og continued the tale.

'So today I was sent up to Maryburgh on the old track, to warn them of the ships attempting to land and Hamish was my contact man.'

At the mention of his name, Hamish's eyes opened wide for a second, but as he realised he was in no danger, he closed them again.

'Hamish told me that a relief column was due at the fort, and they were already coming over the hills. We needed to get word up to the prince, and that's when we set off.

'We used Angus's old trick with the garron. I'd ride fast for two miles and leave the garron and start walking. When Hamish gets to it, he then rides it for a couple of miles and leaves it for me. We made good time and stood a better chance against attack. It was just Hamish's bad luck to be the one that was spotted. I wasn't close but I heard the shot and caught up, and got him onto the horse, and we made a run for it. That's when we turned for Ruthven, in case they wanted to track the horse, but we tried to keep away from soft ground.'

Suddenly, Anghie burst through the door. The urgent expression on his face already told them the news was bad, and before a word was uttered Ian Og and Hamish were on their feet.

'There are two of them at least, and they're looking at the horse. I think they're coming up the brae.'

'Lord save us,' said Sarah, trying to think clearly. 'Ian Og, you go. I'll take care of the rest. Anghie, go and bring the horse to the byre and scold it for being lost.'

Ian Og kissed his sister. 'I shouldn't have stayed. Be careful, Sarah.'

Hamish too was making haste, gathering up his own sword and getting ready to follow Ian Og but Sarah held him back.

'You'll be too slow, and I have an idea.' She opened the door to the other room, holding him close to her so that they avoided disturbing the younger family members sleeping there. They tiptoed to the foot of Grannie Morag's bed.

'Get down on the floor,' she whispered, pulling the cover over to hide him. 'Don't let Grannie see you. When she wakes, you climb in beside her.'

Then she threaded her way back to the door with a soothing 'shh' to a small murmur from one of the girls.

Only the bannock and potato crumbs betrayed the evening's meal, and a quick wipe with her plaid soon disposed of them. The bloodied rag she'd used on Hamish wouldn't burn easily, so Sarah threw it behind the sods of peat. When Anghie almost fell in through the door again, she was sitting at the spinning wheel looking towards the fire.

'Whist,' she said. 'Don't wake Grannie. Did you get Sneeshan this time, Anghie?' Then she turned and clasped her hands to her chest with fright, when she saw the two men behind him. 'Who are you? What do you want?'

The stony faced soldiers glanced around the room.

'*We saw them come in here,*' growled the first man.

Sarah thought quickly. '*I not ... speak ... Scots. What want?*'

'*Two men ... We saw them come here.*'

'*What men?*' She looked worried and was obviously scared. '*Not men. Go away.*'

This might have been an explanation or a request, but neither of the two men took any notice.

'*They're here. They've got to be. That's the horse. You look in there and I'll look here.*'

As the younger man went to open the door, Sarah called out loudly in protest.

'No, no. Not there, please.'

It acted like a spur and before she could reach and stop him, he burst the door open with a great clatter. He couldn't see what was inside, but he heard the startled yells of the young ones and shouted at them. They didn't understand the words but they knew the meaning, and abruptly there was dead silence.

45

Grannie was well accustomed to the darkness of her own room. Awoken suddenly, she saw a stranger framed in the doorway. Her fragile peace was shattered. Deep within her a cauldron of rage overflowed, and a tide of malediction erupted. The voice was ancient and thin, but distress gave it strength and penetration, and each word was like a knife thrust through the eardrums and down into the vitals. It was the soldier's turn not to understand the words, but he knew he was being damned into a black and terrifying eternity.

As the old woman rose from her bed and awkwardly took faltering steps towards him, he backed away. When she grabbed his wrist with skeletal fingers, he jumped with shock and thrust her back into the darkness. His retreat was as swift as his legs could be made to work and he slammed the door, holding it tightly to keep that penetrating voice from piercing his soul.

'Let's get out of here. There's no one in there except little brats and that old witch.'

His friend was made of stronger stuff. *'They're no trouble to us.'*

Ignoring the noise, he upended the bracken-filled sack that made up Anghie's bed, and pulled at Sarah's bed too. He went to scatter the peat pile and stopped short.

'Wait a minute now. Maybe we've found something here.' He grabbed the blood-soaked linen cloth and held it to the light of the fire. Grannie's curses still rang through each crack in the door.

'What's this?' The older man held up the cloth in a bunched fist and thrust it under Sarah's nose.

Anghie started up from the corner into which he had been thrown, but was easily swatted back down by the man's fist.

'Leave her alone,' he shouted. 'She's done nothing.'
As the two men stood over the girl, they didn't realise that the vitriolic tirade had stopped. Grannie opened the door. In a brief moment of clarity, she slowly stepped into the tableau. In Scots, she said scornfully.

'*You men … You wifes … You girls …. This happens.*'
She took the cloth and carefully folded it and gave it to Sarah with a shake of her head. '*She washes. You go. Not right be here. I sleep now.*'

Then she turned back into the room where the white faces of Wee Jimmy and the twins were just visible in the darkness, light glistening on tear-filled eyes. She swept them back into the small room, closed the door and the ancient voice began to pray, 'In the name of the Father, the Son and the Holy Ghost.'

Childish voices could be heard quivering, 'Amen.'

It was a moment or two before the older soldier found his voice. '*Come on. They've gone. There's nothing here but that mad old woman.*'

'*What about the girl?*'

'*Leave her be. Whoever those men are, they're not in here. I'll stick with the horse in the barn till dawn, and you can go and tell the sergeant. And I'll make sure none of these ones go and warn anybody.*'

When the door was safely closed behind the two intruders, Sarah put her finger to her lips. Anghie didn't need such a warning. He knew the soldiers would listen for a while. He certainly would do so if the positions were reversed. He piled the peat up neatly and set about straightening the room.

From the other room came the familiar cadences of the rosary, its comforting lilt calming Grannie and the children. Slowly, Sarah opened the door. 'They've gone.'

The younger ones chattered with relief and rushed to Sarah for comfort, and to see what damage had been wrought. Conscientiously, Grannie, who was kneeling, continued her prayer until the current decade of Hail Marys was completed.

'I'm thirsty,' she said. It was like a demand from another of the children seeking attention. She stood up and came through to join the others, and then she whispered into Sarah's ear. 'There's a man in my bed.'

'I know, Grannie, but it's a secret,' Sarah whispered back.

'Won't the others know?'

'We won't tell them.'

'It's not Granddad, is it?'

'No, Grannie. It's a secret.'

'Right.'

This seemed to satisfy the old woman for the moment. 'I'm still thirsty.'

Anghie brought bowls to the table and everyone had ale except Hamish, who now lay fast asleep in Grannie's bed.

CHAPTER 5

WHEN HE LEFT THE CROFT, Ian Og trusted that Anghie and Sarah would delay any pursuit, and he stole quickly away, heading for the Keppoch area. Even though it was still dark, the full moon gave sufficient light to guide his path. He kept his ears open for any unfamiliar noise that might alert him to the presence of more soldiers. With food in his belly, Ian Og made good time over the mountain tracks he knew so well. It was a pity he'd had to leave Sneeshan behind, but once he crossed the river there wasn't much further to go.

He kept going through the night and although a hint of autumn was in the air, the sun was still rising early. It was getting light as he approached Roy Bridge, where he almost tripped over three men sitting in the heather. The youngest appeared to be about Dadda's age, but he had only one leg and beside him lay a crutch. The other two were older, and scrambled to their feet when they saw him.

'What do you want?' asked the oldest. There was

authority in his voice which time had not eroded.

'I have a message for Keppoch and the prince.'

A dog barked in the distance.

'I'm afraid you've wasted your journey.' The same man spoke again.

'I've got to see someone. I have news.'

'Well, you can't. There's nobody here but the women and us. Everyone else has gone.'

Ian Og sighed. 'Where are they gone? I have to get a message to the prince.'

'Didn't you know? They are already on their way south heading towards Blair Castle and Stirling.'

His heart dropped. 'I've been on the go since yesterday morning and it's urgent.' With a heavy sigh, he added, 'I'll just have to keep going.'

'I'm sorry. There's nothing we can do.' The old man pointed down to the edge of the river. 'Take that path. It should get you there quickest, but you'll have to hurry. Yon man has a great turn of speed on him. They're finding it hard enough to keep up with him.'

'Thanks.' Ian Og turned towards the path.

Suddenly, the man on the ground called after him. 'Wait! Wait a minute.' He lifted a hand to his companions and they pulled him up. 'What about John Cameron's sheltie?' He looked Ian Og up and down. 'This lad wouldn't be too big.'

The others paused to consider this and the spokesman nodded slowly. 'Aye, John will be heading for Stirling. Probably wouldn't be sorry to have it down there. He can carry a lot of stuff.'

'There's only one problem.' The man with the crutch said with a wry smile.

Together they chorused. 'Margaret!' and each shook his head.

The one-legged man explained. 'She can be a terror. Last time I met her she clouted me for keeping John away from home when there were jobs to be done.'

'An awful woman,' agreed the oldest. 'But then, a young lad on a job for the prince? That might make a difference.'

'Aye, she was awfully taken with the prince,' the one-legged man agreed.

'Right enough, yon prince is bonnie. Maybe John would need to watch out for this young Chevalier fellow here, charming Margaret.'

With this, the third man tittered coyly into his hand and spoke. 'I think it would be more likely this young Chevalier fellow would be the one who'd need to watch out!'

Ian Og joined the laughter this provoked, and soon it was agreed that he should accompany the oldest of the three down to the imperious Margaret to ask for the pony. As they started down the path, Ian Og, tired and hungry, tried to gather up his resolution for the journey ahead.

When they reached Margaret's house, his companion left swiftly. Ian Og couldn't believe that the plump apple-cheeked woman smiling sweetly at him was the termagant the men had described. Learning of his mission on behalf of the prince, she needed no persuasion to give him the use of the beast. She placed soup and a couple of bannocks before him on the table, and as he supped, Margaret asked about the action at Fort William and down at Corran. When he was finished, she gave him a twist of screwed-up paper.

'This is for John,' she said. 'He likes a wee sup of tea. And,' she added quietly, 'it keeps him off the drink for a while.'

Soon Ian Og was on his way again. The Shetland pony was short but sturdy, and although Ian Og had to lift his legs sometimes to clear the tufted heather, it bore him well. The encounter had delayed him, and he was concerned that his mount would not cover the ground as quickly as a larger animal, but its gait was deceptive and they made steady progress along the winding trail.

Back at the croft, it took time for everyone to settle down, and sleep was elusive. When it became light, only Hamish and Grannie Morag still lay asleep, snuggled together like spoons. Around the breakfast table the others discussed what they should do. Eventually, it was decided that the twins would go out to the byre and see to Sneeshan. They were too small to harness her, but could assemble tools and straps, and if the soldiers were still nearby, they would be the least suspicious-looking members of the family.

Creel baskets stood waiting for a fine day like this one, and the horse would be a blessing for collecting a good load or two of the peat they'd all been cutting up on the moorland bog. Much of it would be dry by now and ready to be brought into shelter. Normally it meant many hard days, with backs bowed under creaking laden creels, skin rubbed raw, aching shoulders and hands straining to hold coarse heather ropes in place. Sneeshan's assistance was an opportunity not to be missed.

'I can't see anyone,' Anghie said as he craned his neck left and right out the door.

The two girls were delighted with their roles, and set about their chore without the threats or bribes that often accompanied daily tasks. Slowly they made their way along the side of the house, all the time looking to see if they could spot any soldiers. Anghie and Wee

Jimmy, watching their progress from the low doorway, urged them on with nods, until they disappeared around the corner. At the entrance to the byre the two girls stopped.

Morag peeped around the corner and saw Sneeshan tied to the post. Eileen didn't want to miss anything and came past her sister to take a look at the animal. Sneeshan's eyes rolled at these small strangers and she snorted. Promptly, the two moved out of her sight to consider their next move. They were used to the garrons Uncle Angus brought, but this one didn't look very friendly. To Morag's eyes, the beast looked quite mean and thin, which gave her an idea.

'C'mon.'

She pulled her sister away and told her what was required.

A few moments later both girls ventured back into the byre and were greeted in a more friendly way by the tethered beast. The clumps of fresh grass they held more than bought her affection and Morag began to untie the hungry horse. It was Sneeshan's appreciative bellow that woke the sleeping soldier.

He was the elder of yesterday's two unwelcome visitors. Being senior, he'd sent his companion to inform the sergeant where they were and what was happening. He'd decided to watch the house himself so that no one would escape, and he'd maintained his surveillance within the warm dark shelter of the byre, propped up in the darkest corner where he could watch the horse as well, until sleep had overcome him.

With a sudden alertness to banish any consideration that his attention had been elsewhere, he raised the musket which lay beside him and sighted it on Eileen who was feeding Sneeshan clumps of green grass, and quietly discussing the day's work with her.

'Get away from that horse.'

The voice was harsh and made both Sneeshan and Eileen jump with surprise. Tears of fright welled up in the little girl's eyes, and she stood frozen as the animal fidgeted unhappily, hooves scraping at the earth. Morag hadn't seen the figure either and was just as startled as her sister, but remembering her instructions, stroked the horse reassuringly.

'There, there,' she said. She carefully held the strap at the horse's head, hoping the garron had no strange character quirks that might lead her to bite.

'Leave the horse.' The man was more insistent, but somewhat disconcerted by the small size of the opposition.

Morag didn't know what to do next. 'We ... have to work,' she said very clearly, but there came no response to that.

Raising his weapon at Eileen, the soldier said, 'Go ... get ... big sister.'

Dropping the last morsel of grass, Eileen scampered out of the byre.

The soldier immediately swung his musket towards Morag. *'Leave that horse.'*

She shut her eyes tightly and grimly held onto Sneeshan, grateful for her warm steady presence. Morag vaguely understood the word for horse, but waited, stock still, and prayed that Sarah would come quickly to the rescue.

The others were waiting at the croft door when Eileen came running towards them, calling, 'Sarah! Sarah! There's a soldier! Come quick! Quick!'

She took Sarah's hand and started to pull, but the

urging was hardly necessary as they ran the few paces to the byre entrance. Anghie unsuccessfully tried to stop Wee Jimmy from following.

The tableau was still in place when Sarah entered the dark shelter. Morag had gingerly opened one eye once she realised that the stranger was not going to shoot her straight away. With the sound of Sarah's pounding feet coming to a halt in front of her, she opened the other.

'Sarah, Sarah, tell him not to shoot me,' she squeaked.

'It's all right.' Sarah said, raising her palm towards her in a calming gesture. Then to the soldier, with a confidence she was not feeling, she said, '*She is girl little. What you do? Go away. We work now.*'

She wasn't sure if her Scots made sense, or how much Gaelic he might understand, so she began to mime lifting up the creels and fastening them on the horse.

Morag, hardly daring to breathe and mesmerised by the musket still aimed at her, held the horse's head, patting her neck. Although Sarah was daunted, she was starting to lift up the peat creel when Wee Jimmy ran into the byre, and stopped abruptly at the sight.

This was ammunition the soldier could not withstand. The three, Morag, Eileen and Wee Jimmy, hair unkempt, plaids ragged, dirty and awry, with tear-filled eyes, melted him. He had young ones of his own of about the same ages. He lowered his musket.

With a look of relief, Sarah lifted up the peat creels and began to strap them into place. '*We work now.*'

'*I'm afraid not.*' The weary family man shook his head. '*Not work.*' he said. '*Stay in the house.*' And he pushed Morag gently away from Sneeshan and shooed them out of the byre as he followed them.

At the front of the croft, Anghie waited anxiously

in the doorway, where he had been bidden to stay by Sarah.

A thought struck the soldier. *'Wait a minute.'* He turned towards the croft and pulled Anghie out of the way. *'I want to take another look.'*

Now that it was daylight, the little house could be more easily inspected. The main room showed signs of an early meal: bowls still streaked with brose, and bannock crumbs on the floor. He carefully opened the wee room. It smelt stale, full of tired body odour. The bed spaces were all empty now except Grannie's. She was lying untidily, her head back, mouth open, snoring and showing ancient remnants of teeth. It was a regular grunt of a snore. When the soldier's foot kicked the end of her bed, the noise stopped abruptly.

'What's that?' asked the old woman, her voice pitched high. 'Who's that?' she called in a sharper tone, and peered out from under the mound of coverings. The man retreated quickly. He had no wish to call down upon himself the fluent Celtic wrath of the old witch. As he shut the door, the voice was rising higher. Grateful to escape her curses, he pushed past Anghie, out into the fresh air.

Across the heather the other soldier was on his way back and waved an acknowledgement. The two met each other just out of sight of the house.

'What do you think?' inquired the younger man.

He shook his head. *'Long gone now if they were ever here.'*

'It's the horse. I'm sure it's the same horse.'

'How can we tell? There's no sign of anyone now but the children. They won't be doing us much harm.'

'That oldest one, she could do me some harm any day.'

'Are you mad? If she didn't put a knife into you, she'd

put a spell on you. They're all witches. What about the old woman last night?'

The pair moved down the brae muttering together, their retreat watched with relief by Sarah and the rest of the family.

CHAPTER 6

IT WAS A PITY THEY couldn't get up to the peat bog this fine morning, but at least they were all safe. Hamish would have to stay in Grannie's bed for another hour or two. The old lady loved the intrigue.

'I fooled him,' she whispered to her young companion as she snuggled down again.

'You did indeed, Grannie,' mumbled the young man.

Outside, Anghie was watching the men depart. 'What do they want?'

'I don't know,' Sarah shook her head. 'And why would they be here in Glen Rowan? Nobody ever comes here. They obviously followed the tracks of Ian Og and Hamish. They're up to no good anyway.'

'How can we stop them?' said Morag.

'I don't know,' Sarah said, pausing as she thought about it, and then in a purposeful voice. 'We have plenty to do in the meantime.'

Amid moans and groans she set the family to their daily tasks. Reluctantly they turned to their jobs, but none were engrossed. When Sarah began to ponder aloud, they made no more pretence and gathered around the table again.

'We're not strong enough to fight them,' she said.

'There are other ways.' Anghie was itching to strike a blow against the government's men. 'We can lame the horses.'

'They probably haven't got many horses. And besides, how could we get near enough?'

'We could dig a big pit for them to fall into.' With this, Eileen provoked argument, and each of them came up with even wilder ideas.

'We're not much of an army.' Sarah shook her head. 'We still don't know how many soldiers there are. We need to know what's happening.'

'We could go and look,' offered the two girls.

'You'd be spotted in a minute.' Anghie was scornful. 'I'd better go.'

'No, wait a minute.' Sarah was trying to consider the right course of action. 'They'll be looking out for someone as big as you, and whatever happens we need to have a man here.'

Despite the hyperbole in the comment, it was true that Anghie was now the man of the croft and he agreed with Sarah's point.

'I could go.' Wee Jimmy was almost jumping up and down with excitement. Sarah told him to be quiet, but she mulled over his suggestion.

'Well now … That's not such a bad idea.' As the rest frowned at Jimmy, she turned instead to Eileen. 'You're the one to go. Keep out of sight, but go and see what those soldiers are doing.' Only a blind man could have missed the complete deflation of the boy, so reluctantly Sarah added, 'And you can take Jimmy with you. He'll be your messenger,' she added. 'And he has to do as he's told by you. This is very important.' Both nodded with enormous smiles of satisfaction splitting their faces. 'But mind and be careful now, BOTH of you.'

Taking to the task with a will, Eileen and Jimmy scurried out the door and made for the scrub beside the track. There was little cover until the ash trees, but the two carefully wove their way between the bracken and heather, and Sarah watched them anxiously till they were lost to sight.

It wasn't long before Jimmy returned crouching as he ran. 'Eileen says there are twenty-five or thirty soldiers and they're just standing around.'

'What does that mean?'

'I don't know. They're just standing around. Looks like they're waiting for something.'

'What can they be waiting for?' Sarah wondered.

'They're talking sort of quiet, but we don't know what they're saying.'

'You get back to Eileen. And be careful, mind. Keep out of sight. Let us know if there's any change.'

By now Grannie had risen. For fifty years or more, her day had begun with the same routine. Using the smallest and oldest pot, she scooped water from the bucket, or if there was some already heating over the fire, she used that. Then the little pot, black from years of peat tar, was placed onto the embers of the fire. She had her own way of doing this, and very quickly air circulated and reddened the fire.

She added a large pinch of tea before she set out, either for the midden behind the house, or when the weather was better, for the little stream that ran into the main river further down the glen. There was a quiet spot she used, sheltered by bushes and rowan trees, where she could squat and relieve herself into the water. It sometimes took her a while but she liked this moment of peace.

On this day, when Grannie was squatting by the burn, she caught sight of a rider galloping over the hill from Glengarry. He was dressed in a plaid that flapped about him, and rode a heavy soldier's horse. The old woman stayed quiet and still. Her memory might have faded, but her long habits of suspicion had not. She waited until he was out of sight before she rose.

No one expected Grannie to bring in the news that a messenger had come.

'Are you sure, Grannie?' asked Sarah.

'Of course I'm sure. I'm not doting yet.' She sniffed and took a sup of the black tea, then smacked her lips appreciatively. 'He was a big lout of a man on a big horse. A soldier, I tell you. He might have come from Gairlochy or even Invergarry. There's something afoot.'

As Hamish came limping in from the wee room, he heard this lucid speech and like the others was astonished. The events of the night had somehow opened a window within the old woman. If it stayed with her, she would be a powerful addition against any foe.

Hungrily, Hamish feasted on a bowl of barley porridge, as they discussed the likely movements of the government men. When Wee Jimmy scampered in with the news that a horseman had arrived, and the soldiers were getting ready to move out, he was disappointed to find out that they already knew.

Soon, Eileen returned and confirmed that the group was heading northwards.

'That's their best way to the Corrieyairack pass,' said Hamish. 'I'll get the horse and make a run to tell the highlanders that they're likely to meet trouble.'

'Too late for that,' said Sarah. 'We have to think of a way to stop them here.'

Grannie supped her tea and filled her pipe and let the others discuss the best means to stop the men. Each scheme was wilder than the last. Driving the cattle at them would mean gathering all the cattle, a day's work itself. Riding to Glen Roy or Spean Bridge to get help would also take too long.

Grannie looked up from her last sup of tea. 'Set fire to them,' she said and smacked her lips.

For a moment Sarah thought she had reverted to foolishness, but Grannie said it again. 'Set fire to them. Burn them off the hill.'

It took only a moment or two for this idea to sink in.

'Yes,' Sarah said excitedly. 'We don't have to kill them, just delay them, and if we do it right they'll be too far away to take it out on us.'

Ever practical, Anghie pointed out, 'There are cattle on the west hill. They'll have to come back over the burn ... and there's sheep and goats near the peat bog.' He was thinking quickly. 'If we herded them into the wetter ground, we could save them later.'

'We could do that, couldn't we?' Eileen and Wee Morag volunteered together.

'We'll get the cattle to the bog first and then the other animals. We'll need the sheep dog and Wee Jimmy. He's good with the animals.'

'Right ... You get cracking with that,' said Sarah. Then looking at Hamish and Anghie, she added, 'And we three will get the heather burning.'

'And don't forget me.' Grannie insisted on going with Anghie. 'It's my idea and I am not being stuck here, if there's work to be done.'

Morag, Eileen and Wee Jimmy began to drag barley

and oatmeal sacks up to the shelter of the old sheep fank. Into this pen they dumped the sacks in two of Uncle Angus's barrels hidden there. Then they went looking for the livestock.

Wee Jimmy soon returned with news that they'd seen men making their way along the hill track, but the twins felt there was still time to guide the cattle to safety. They were likely to be browsing close to each other, and should be easy to drive down to the water. Sheep were much more likely to scatter themselves over the hillside, so they'd taken the dog to stop them spreading out all over the bog.

While it might be hard to herd the animals, there should be enough time before any fire reached them. If trouble came, Wee Jimmy and the twins could always shelter safely up at the whisky still.

Grannie and Anghie were not far behind the soldiers and were staying out of sight. They carried a lanthorn, tinderbox, pine sticks and suet candles, and were whispering three times over all the decades of the rosary. It would take nearly an hour. By then the soldiers would have covered quite a distance from the croft, and that would be the time to start firing the bracken and heather to cut off any retreat.

It would be tricky work for the two of them because once the fire was lit there was no means to control it. The wind should carry it to the soldiers, or back up the track if its direction changed. In either case, it would become a barrier. Grannie and Anghie had to work carefully so that they could gain the safety of one of the hillside streams. Fortunately, Grannie's old body was spry enough, but Anghie knew he would have to keep a watchful eye on her.

For the injured Hamish riding bareback with Sarah

on Sneeshan, the task was to circle around and set fire to the ground at the head of the glen. If they could cut off the escape to Glen Roy, the soldiers would have to move back towards Wade's road, and whatever plans they'd had would be foiled.

The fire had to be broad enough and long enough to make the track impassable for a few hours at least, but they didn't want the soldiers to realise what was happening before the flames took hold. It meant working quickly and remaining out of sight. The pair rode earnestly. Sneeshan must have known her efforts were important and she did not falter. Within an hour they were about three miles ahead of their quarry on the western side of the track.

To hurry their task, Sarah had brought a pot of smouldering peat as well as pine sticks, heather stems, tinder and flint and a lanthorn. She slid off the horse while Hamish kindled the pine sticks and heather stems, and threw them down towards the nimble Sarah who set the fires in place.

Some flared up quickly and others smouldered, but the pair moved on steadily, trusting that the dry leaves and old bracken would do the work for them. With a trail of small fires behind them, they finally sought rest and shelter for themselves on a rocky scree slope, and settled down to wait and see the results of their efforts.

CHAPTER 7

WHILE THE FAMILY IN THE glen was preparing to delay the soldiers, Ian Og and the tiny sheltie that carried him finally reached the trampled grass and muddy trail of the clansmen. The path became much easier to follow and he approached Blair Castle shortly after noon.

Before him there was a large gathering of men. Some stood, but mostly they were sitting or squatting on the ground, obviously waiting for something to happen. Smoke from damp wood hung lazily over several smouldering fires. Through the crowd he guided his pony towards the big house and didn't notice friendly waves on his left, nor did he hear the yells of Dadda, Ranald and Roderick when he approached the pair of sentries guarding the entrance to the castle.

The men watched as he dismounted, stumbling for a moment with the stiffness in his legs. Fortunately, Roderick came up behind him and put a steadying arm around his shoulders. Ian Og handed him the reins.

'He belongs to John Cameron of Glen Nevis.'

'I'll see to him,' his uncle said, but Ian Og was already telling the sentries he had an urgent message for the prince.

'There was hardly a pause before they answered. 'Sorry, friend. We can't just let you in unless you've got the password.'

'The password? What password?' Ian Og was confused by the request. 'I don't know any password. I've got an urgent message for the prince from Onich.'

'Onich, you say.' The sentry's tone made it clear that news from Onich could not be important enough to disturb anyone.

'You must be the fifth in the last few minutes, all wanting to see the prince urgently. We can't let any old traveller in.'

'Look,' Ian Og was too tired to banter. 'I have to see someone. It's urgent. Is Glengarry, Locheil or anybody else in there I can talk to?'

'You'll have to wait over there with the others. They're all urgent.' He waved a hand down towards some trees. 'We've been told not to let anyone through here till we get further orders. You could be a spy.'

'Don't be daft.' Roderick was still there, holding the reins. 'Look at him! He's nearly out on his feet. He's not a spy.'

'I can't help that. They've put a price on his head.'

'What?' Ian Og could make no sense of this.

'Yes, the king in London.'

'Has done what?'

'Put a price on the prince's head.'

It still obviously meant nothing to the exhausted young man before him, so the sentry addressed the uncle instead. 'You know ... a bounty.'

'The King put a bounty on his own cousin?' Dadda

had joined the group and was astonished.

'Yes. It's terrible, I know, so that's why we can't let you through.'

This might have satisfied Dadda and Roderick, who began to pull Ian Og back, but he shrugged off their kindly hands and soundly addressed the man. 'Look, I have to see someone. What about Alistair? Alistair would get me to the prince, I know he would.'

'I doubt it. Nobody is getting through just now.'

In rage and frustration, Ian Og looked up to the sky and called, 'Alistair Glic! Where are you when I need you?'

The response was as if he had cast a magic spell.

'Alistair ... you mean Alistair Glic? Are you one of his men? Why didn't you say so?' His tone was warmer now. 'I'll send the boy for him. You're still in for a wait, though. There's a crowd of people inside all waiting too.'

'So how did you get yourself into that state?' Roderick asked while they waited.

Ian Og told them of the ambush and flight to Glen Rowan, and how he left the others to deal with the soldiers. The watch keepers were listening too, and having decided he was not a government assassin, shared a bannock with the young messenger who chewed thoughtfully and took sips of whisky from Dadda's horn cup. He told of his long run over the hills, before Margaret had given him the little sheltie.

There was silence when he finished. It was broken by the arrival of an embroidered and be-laced vision, which came running eagerly from the house to clasp the ragged Ian Og and hug him with joy. The two sentries smiled with relief. Dadda and the uncles watched with pride and concern.

'Ian Og!' said Alistair with delight. 'You're just the man. And you've got news from Onich?'

Ian Og's weariness seemed to have fallen off him with the embrace of his friend.

'Aye, it was great. We managed to hold off three supply ships bound for the fort. They were heading back down the loch when I left, but we'll need more munitions for the cannons, to be ready for them when they come back.'

'Good man.' Alistair drew him towards the house then turned back to the family.

'I'll look after him and see he gets fed.'

'And don't forget the horse. It's John Cameron's,' Ian Og added.

The Glen Rowan men were quiet until they were alone. Soon each had a suggestion. Should they leave now and rejoin the army further along its path; maybe find Donald Keppoch and tell him what had occurred; perhaps get a body of men together?

A moment later, Angus rode in on his ever-faithful Pepper. 'Look!' said Dadda and called out to his brother-in-law. 'Angus! We're over here.' While Pepper picked her way through the crowd, Dadda had a thought. 'I wonder if he knows anything about the soldiers in the glen. He'll want to help.'

Meanwhile, up at the big house, inside the door, Ian Og took hold of Alistair's arm.

'I have bad news as well.'

His friend made a face. 'We don't need any more bad news at the moment. You'd better let me have it first.'

'Campbell of Inverawe brought men up the west road into the fort, and later more of his men came that way to join him. We don't know whether they came because they'd got word we were getting ready to attack, or just as a precaution.'

'You're sure of this?' By now they were in a large room filled with people standing in groups and talking loudly. There was a sudden hush as they turned and stared at the newcomer before returning to their discussions.

'Yes,' Ian Og nodded when the noise level rose again. 'I went up to tell our people in Maryburgh about the boats, and Hamish was coming to you with the news. We got ambushed on the way.'

Alistair stopped at another door. 'Is Hamish all right?'

'I hope so. Sarah's looking after him, but I'm worried.'

'Come on,' said Alistair, knocking gently. 'We'd better get it over with.'

'What?'

'Your report to Locheil, he needs to know, good or bad.'

Before he realised what was happening, Ian Og was being ushered into the largest room he'd ever seen. His first thought was that the table was nearly as big as the family's croft. Untidily around it were several large chairs, with seats padded in rich brocade. Maps and papers covered the table and delft plates held down their curled edges.

Locheil looked tired as he slumped in one of the chairs. Young Glengarry, replacing his father who had gone to pledge support to the enemy General Cope, was also red-eyed, but sat straight, while the third person in the room, a young man, glowing with energy, jabbed at one of the maps with a long white finger. It was Bonnie Prince Charles himself.

'Your Highness, this is the messenger.' Alistair bowed low with one leg elegantly placed in front of him.

Ian Og didn't know what he was supposed to do but bowed his head respectfully.

'Have you news, boy?' Locheil spoke. 'Tell us the news.'

Ian Og cleared his throat nervously and began. 'We held off three supply ships at Corran Narrows, the day before yesterday.' As he spoke, Locheil translated some of the words into French for the prince.

It was quite clear, however, that the prince understood what had been said as he banged the table with his clenched fist in a gesture of satisfaction. '*C'est ça,*' and in Gaelic he added, 'I knew it!'

Alistair coughed politely and the men looked at him. 'There is more,' he said, and nodded to Ian Og to continue.

'When I came back through Maryburgh, I learned that a second group of Campbell's men had arrived at the fort. Hamish was coming to tell you this. We set off immediately for Spean, but were ambushed along the way, which is why I have been delayed several hours.'

The prince nodded thoughtfully as the translation ended. Locheil and Glengarry both rose and stood looking down at the maps on the table. Slowly, the prince spoke in Gaelic and tapped one of the charts. 'So it's definite. We'll face Cope at Stirling or Perth. No point in dividing the forces if the fort is well reinforced.'

Alistair made another bow to the backs of the three men, and with a slight jerk of his head nodded towards the door. It was time to withdraw. As Ian Og bowed his head respectfully, the prince's returned his attention to him. He spoke slowly.

'Well done, warrior. What is name?'

To be addressed directly in this way so surprised Ian Og that it was a moment before the words could escape.

'Ian Og MacDonell of Glen Rowan, Sire.'

The prince smiled graciously. 'Ian Og MacDonell of Glen Rowan, this news important. Well done. You are good warrior.'

With a rapid tug he tore off a button from his waistcoat and lobbed it towards Ian Og who caught it with both hands.

'This to thank you,' said the prince.

He turned back to look at the maps. As the young man spluttered his gratitude, Alistair drew him firmly out of the room.

'Alistair, look at that. The prince gave it to me. Look, look! It's gold! It's got a lion on it.' The excited young man continued to speak in a torrent of words, about the generosity of the prince as they made their way to the back of the house where food was being prepared, and sat down at a table.

'Sit here and I'll get Anna.' Alistair went to the other end of the room and spoke quietly into the ear of a pretty girl, who smiled. She picked up a jug and two bowls and, with Alistair's friendly arm around her shoulder, came to where Ian Og sat.

'Anna,' said Alistair. 'This man travelled many miles to serve his prince and received a precious gift in reward. Alas, but not as precious as one of your smiles.'

'Oh Alistair!' she said with dimpled cheeks as she filled the bowls and admired the gold trophy held out for her inspection. Seeing the ale flowing from the jug, Ian Og became overwhelmed with thirst. He greedily drained his bowl even before Alistair's was filled.

'I think,' said Alistair to Anna, 'some food might be needed as well. Can you do something for him?'

'I'm all right,' Ian Og lied.

Alistair ignored his words and when the girl smiled assent, he turned again to his friend. 'Anna will look after you while I go and see what the orders are.'

The sound of bustle within the house, the muffled shouts and running feet outside, suggested an army was getting ready to move again.

Ian Og supped the broth which kind-hearted Anna put before him, and stuffed the accompanying bannock into his sporran as he yawned with tiredness. Alistair soon returned. This time, the lace was gone and he was dressed as a highlander, still looking magnificent with tan jacket, loose linen shirt and plaid, fine trews and stout buckled brogues.

'We're off again!' he said excitedly. 'It's Perth and General Cope. Your information clinched it. As soon as you've rested, Locheil says you've to get yourself back to Corran and keep us up to date on what's happening.'

It was this news that brought Ian Og up short. The excitement of seeing the prince and the activity around him had driven other considerations from his mind.

'Oh, Lord save us. I have to get back to Glen Rowan first. The soldiers were there when I left. I have to get back and help the others.'

He stood up and would have made for the door, but Alistair held him.

'Wait! Wait! What happened?'

It was all Alistair could do to hold Ian Og long enough to get more details of the ambush and the flight to Glen Rowan with Hamish. He was shocked when he heard that two soldiers had followed them to the croft. Although sounds of activity outside were gradually increasing, neither paid heed to it. Alistair let out his breath in a long tuneless half-whistle and, shaking his head, said, 'No wonder you're anxious to get back. Wait here for me and I'll see if I can get some help. Everybody's moving out, so I don't know how long I'll be. Don't go without seeing me.'

Reluctantly, Ian Og sat down again. He meant to stay alert, but sleep soon overwhelmed him, the gold button clasped tightly in his hand.

A while later Anna was shaking him. 'Sorry to wake you. I have to go home now. Alistair saw you asleep and told me to tell you not to worry. Everything'll be all right.'

Ian Og was still half-asleep. He rubbed his eyes and peered blearily around him but couldn't immediately make sense of his surroundings.

'Alistair,' the girl emphasised. 'He said to tell you it would be all right.'

'Alistair!' Realisation dawned on him. He jumped to his feet, startling the girl, who took a couple of steps backwards. 'Where is he?'

'He's gone. They've all gone.'

'How long have I been sleeping here?'

'I don't know … perhaps an hour or so.'

'Oh Lord. I have to go … the family!'

'He said to let you sleep and tell you everything would be all right.'

Ian Og was struggling to think straight. 'And he left with the prince?' he asked.

'Yes, I think so. I brought you a couple of pancakes that were left over.' Shyly, she proffered him the food.

Even in his befuddled state, he was not immune to a pretty girl, but it was hard to smile as he thrust the gift into his sporran.

'Thank you, Anna. You're very kind but I have to go,' he said. 'Why did he leave me?'

'I'm sorry,' she said as she turned away. 'I don't know.'

Out in the open air, Ian Og paused and looked around him. There was no one left but the women of the house. The fires still smouldered but all the men were gone, south towards Perth. A great emptiness seeped into his soul. He took a deep breath and sniffed, trying to stop the tears from welling. The journey would be hard enough without that. Even though his legs were stiff and sore from his efforts since he left the croft, there was no choice. He must start running again. It would be too late anyway: whatever was to happen would have already taken place.

He took a few steps, but thoughts of everyone at home overwhelmed him, and the dam of tears burst. There were no sentries now, but where they had stood, he stopped for a moment. 'God help them,' he prayed and with a final determined sniff, wiped his eyes with the end of his plaid and began to retrace his steps towards home.

He had only taken a few more paces when, as far as he was concerned, a miracle occurred. Before him, browsing patiently, almost hidden in the shelter of the trees where Uncle Roderick had loosely tied him, was the Shetland pony and a pile of grass. There was no sign of anyone else. Whatever had happened to John Cameron, he hadn't spotted his little steed.

'I'll call you Angel, because that's what you are,' said Ian Og sniffing his tears back and mounting the little beast again. Clearly, it was an omen that he was meant to return home. Now with Angel, his heart lifted. He turned north and let her find her own path towards home.

As Angel daintily picked her way along the track, all was quiet. For several miles there was no sign of anybody. He began to notice prints in the track ahead of him. Several horses had recently passed this way. It wasn't possible to tell whether they were friend or foe.

He estimated that only foolhardy men would venture into MacDonell country during the uprising. He kicked his heels to make the little horse canter, and although she scampered willingly for a few paces, Angel soon resumed her usual tight trot. The beast was willing enough, but was unaccustomed to travelling long distances at any great speed.

Whoever was making the tracks was in a hurry, and Ian Og could feel the distance between them increasing. There was little point in urging the pony beyond her strength. If that happened they would both be worse off, and would repay Margaret Cameron ill for the trust she had shown.

When the track crossed damp earth, he could make out distinct sets of footprints, and Ian Og felt the men must be very cocky if they made no effort to disguise their route. Because he was tired it took a while before he realised that the direction they were travelling in was very much the same as his own.

At each fork he inspected the ground in the hope they would take another route, but at every turn they were still ahead of him and drawing further away. These must be men hastening to join the soldiers already up in Glen Rowan.

It frustrated him that he could not push any extra

effort from the little Shetland. He didn't want to stop, even to drink. He was so carefully watching the ground before him that he didn't see the man waiting by the side of the track, until a broad arm came out and pulled him off his mount.

Take it easy, boy.' It was Uncle Angus. 'Take it easy and stop struggling. By Jove, you've got some pluck, lad. We realised someone was following us, but you were dead to the world when we left. Never thought it could be you, and you'd have the pony.' He steadied the young man and lowered him to the ground. 'Here, sit and rest for a moment. I told them I'd wait and deal with whoever was following.'

'But Angus, you're supposed to be heading for Stirling.'

The older man shook his head wistfully. 'I know … It's the prince we should be with, but we might do him a good turn in Glen Rowan, and no one will miss us for a couple of days.'

'But you didn't just leave like that? I mean, without telling someone?'

'Oh no, I didn't.' Angus brought some water from a bog pool in the heel of his shoe and Ian Og drank from it.

'Alistair came to find us. He told us what happened to you and Hamish, and how the soldiers had followed you to the croft. That settled it. We all set off for Glen Rowan.'

'You mean Dadda, Alistair and my uncles?'

'Yes.' Angus's big face grinned ruefully. 'The prince can manage Stirling without our help just now, and we can catch up with him later.'

The matter was obviously simple in his uncle's mind, and Ian Og felt reassured. It was as if a big weight had been lifted from his shoulders, and responsibility was easing from his mind. No matter how terrible the situation at home, the family and Alistair would deal with it.

He decided to walk for a while with Angus and give the loyal Angel a much-needed rest, but when exhaustion claimed him, his uncle gently lifted him onto Pepper's back and led the two animals up the slope to the glen.

CHAPTER 8

EVEN BEFORE ALISTAIR, Roderick and Dadda reached the crest of the hill and looked down into Glen Rowan, they could smell the smoke. It was possible to see the snaking line of fire, wide streaks of charred vegetation in its wake, in the smog-enveloped glen.

'Bastards!' said Roderick, scrambling off the back of his garron. 'Those bastards have set fire to the glen.'

He ran ahead towards the croft then stopped with a puzzled look on his face.

'Wait a minute. The place looks untouched.'

He ran in the door. As the others came to a halt, Roderick emerged shaking his head.

'That's strange. Everything is fine, but there's no one here.'

'No sign of life at all? What about Grannie?'

'No, I can't find anyone at all. Maybe they've driven them off ... or even killed them.' He paused. 'The house is fine.'

Alistair was just as puzzled. 'You two search round

here, and I'll go and see what that fire is about. It's not the time to be burning heather.'

Horse and rider cantered along the track, following the path of fresh horse tracks which led straight into the scorched area. As Alistair paused, pondering what to do, there was a distant 'halloo'. Up in the shelter of rocks on the hill, he saw Grannie with Anghie, yelling and waving, flapping arms and pointing further up the glen. These two appeared to be none the worse, so he turned his attention to the barrier in front of him.

There didn't seem to be a path through the charred ground. The fire here had almost burnt itself out by now, but he decided it would be safer for man and beast to skirt around the black expanse. As he rode along the edge of the hill, thick waves of smoke rolled steadily across the ground making visibility difficult. His eyes were stinging, but he rode forward until gradually he could make out the hazy form of men ahead. It took a few moments before he was able to see that the soldiers were almost clear of a great black smoking semicircle of moorland.

This was a raiding party, and large enough to damage the highlanders in the Corrieyairack. Battles hinged on fewer men. Surprise would have been their greatest weapon but the fire had caused them a fatal delay and Alistair shook his head and smiled at the ingenuity of the Glen Rowan family, who had obviously come up with this masterstroke.

There was no time for celebration. It was his task to get word back to the prince. With a final look to assess the number of men and equipment they carried, he turned away. He had no wish to be spotted. When he turned, his attention was caught by a slight movement on the far hillside. There were two figures hiding from the soldiers behind a large rock. Even from this distance, Alistair could recognise Sarah's compact form and dark hair. Hamish must be the ginger-haired man with her, and clearly they did not recognise that the danger lay not with the soldiers eagerly making their escape, but from the fire itself. Red flames were flickering across the path of their retreat. To yell and shout would alert the soldiers, but he had to warn the pair of the dangers they faced.

For Hamish and Sarah, oblivious of the impending danger, the day had gone well. Breathlessly, they peered out from the shelter of the great boulder. They could see the last of the soldiers making the detour westwards. Whatever mischief they were bound upon had been delayed by several hours, and not a shot fired. The croft and family were safe.

'Oh, Hamish,' Sarah's face was sweaty and streaked with soot. 'We did it, we did it! Look at them go!'

'You did most of it,' said Hamish. 'I could only help.'

'Oh, it was wonderful. Did you see them stop?'

They had both watched the column of soldiers gradually bunch up as they realised there was fire both behind and ahead.

Hamish nodded. 'It was good!'

'I had a terrible thought they might come over in this direction.'

'No, you set the fires just right.'

'It worked well. Didn't it?' She clasped him in a great hug of exuberant joy, and craned up and kissed his cheek joyfully.

Hamish was taken by surprise, but despite his quiet ways he was not the shy lad of five years ago. His arms enfolded and held her. The movement was gentle but firm and stopped her stepping away as she had meant to do. She could easily have pushed herself free and the moment would have passed, but a mixture of excitement and curiosity overtook her.

This time, she did not have to crane her neck so much. Hamish bent his face down and kissed her slowly and lovingly full on the lips. The red beard was surprisingly soft against her cheek, and his lips were moist against hers. A tingle rose within her, mixing with the excitement of the afternoon, but she nearly couldn't breathe. Her lungs were bursting. Urgently, she pulled her face away and saw the disappointment in Hamish's eyes. He thought she must dislike the kiss.

'No,' she wheezed. 'I just have to breathe.'

'I didn't think of that.' He smiled and loosened his embrace a little, before he bent to kiss her again.

Sarah closed her eyes and let air pass through her nostrils as they kissed again. Faintly within the smoke she could smell his skin and feel the tickle of his beard and then felt his lips again. His touch was gentle as he began to fondle her breasts, and Sarah could feel her body stir in response, but a vision of Alistair came to her mind. A fire began to spread up and down her spine. When Hamish lightly touched her tongue with his tongue, the shock was like a fist knocking on a massive door and she swiftly pulled away from him.

It was not so easy for Hamish to cool his feelings. He had loved Sarah from the first moment he had met her, and had watched and waited until he felt the time was right to tell her. They were together on a blackened moor at the beginning of a war, and he could not let it pass. He would be away for weeks and wanted to keep her in his heart.

'Oh Sarah … you know I love you. I've always loved you. Don't pull away now.'

'I'm not.' With a thumping heart, she tried to be calm. 'It's just that ...' she couldn't think of a reason.

'You like me. Don't you?'

Slowly, she nodded.

'You didn't mind me kissing you?'

Slowly, she shook her head.

He hadn't loosened his arms and his words were quiet, but she could feel the intense strength and confidence that was hidden within him.

'Kiss me again. It will have to last me a long time.'

Already Sarah knew she had brought this upon herself, and with a nagging reluctance, brought her face up again to meet his.

He misunderstood her caution and strove to make the kiss gentle as he brought her closer. Sarah was burning in a cauldron of mixed emotion: fear, exhilaration, remorse.

This was how Alistair found them. He had travelled across open country into the circle of fire to save them, and there they were behind a rock kissing, oblivious to the dangers all around, especially the soldiers and the flames. His anger erupted.

'What are you doing?' His voice shook and he gave neither time to reply. 'Can't you see the fire?'

Sneeshan jerked at the harsh voice, and pulled at the reins that Hamish had wrapped around his arm.

'Yes. Of course we can,' Hamish said as he released his embrace on Sarah. 'We did it. We stopped them.'

'Yes, and nearly killed everything in the glen.' Alistair's voice grated menacingly.

'Are they all safe? They had plenty of time to get clear. Is it Grannie?' Sarah asked, concerned.

'No, it's NOT Grannie,' Alistair snapped. 'But it could have been.' He didn't care that he was causing pain. He wanted to hurt her.

'Is it Anghie?'

'No.'

'What about Jimmy and the girls?'

'No. But it is no thanks to you two.'

Alistair was saved from further elaboration by the sound of musket fire. The rear guard of the soldiers had seen the lone rider and the pair he was talking to, so they primed their weapons and started shooting.

'Never mind that now. We're all in danger here. The bog up there is catching and we have to go.'

When neither moved, both rooted in shock on the spot, he shouted, 'Now!' and put his hand down for Sarah to grasp. She was up behind him in a moment and he kicked his horse and took off, leaving Hamish to gather his wits and clamber back onto Sneeshan as best he could and follow.

Alistair kicked his horse on at a furious gallop, which soon brought them clear of the smoking circle of fire and out of sight of the soldiers. Abruptly, he reined in.

'Go home,' he said. 'Everyone's there.'

'Aren't you coming?' Sarah asked, sliding obediently off the horse.

'I have to go and warn the prince. They're heading for the Corrieyairack and Cope is on his way. These must have been reinforcements for him.'

'I'm sorry,' she said.

'There's nothing for you to be sorry about.' He was still stern. 'You and Hamish did a very good job. I'll tell the prince how well you did it.'

He didn't smile as he spoke and Sarah could feel her lip begin to tremble. She was determined not to cry in front of him.

'May God keep you,' she said as purposefully as she could, blinking to disperse the liquid beginning to pool in her eyes.

It was a tiny tear escaping which betrayed her, and melted all the anger within the jealous man.

'Oh, Sarah,' he sighed and jumped down from the horse. For the second time that day, she found herself being kissed. This was not a tender embrace, no concern for comfort, but a great physical spark linked them. It was an emotional explosion of man and woman, spreading out from lips and tongue, with no time for maidenly reticence.

As abruptly as he had begun, Alistair stopped. 'Oh dearest Sarah, forgive me.' His arms around her became gentle. 'Please come under the trees and sit with me, so I can tell you what I must tell you before I head off to fight a war.'

When they were sitting together on the ground amongst the trees, and out of sight of the main track they had just ridden down, Alistair took a deep breath.

'I have loved you ever since that day at the fort when you rescued young Peter. Whenever I came to the glen, I watched you grow into a fine young woman. I loved you even more and admired how you became the mother of the family, when Mamma died the night Jimmy was born. It wasn't just with the young ones. Dadda and the uncles came to rely more and more on your kindness and good judgement, and Grannie treated you like her own daughter.'

'Oh, Alistair,' Sarah interrupted. 'Is it the right time to be talking like this?' She paused. 'I don't want you to go off to serve the prince without me telling you that I too remember that day at the fort when we rescued young Peter. You lit a spark in my heart which still burns.'

Alistair gazed adoringly at her. He lightly trailed his fingers down her cheek, over her lips and down her arms. Sarah's skin prickled at his sensual touch. Slowly the two came close and kissed again gently. The mutual love they felt overtook them as they lay back upon the ground, still kissing passionately. Sarah could feel Alistair's hands lift up her plaid, and then fumble at his own kilt as he slowly positioned himself on top of her. She didn't try to resist in any way, and although her mind was racing, she knew she didn't want to resist.

Now she could feel Alistair's naked flesh pressed against hers, and she kissed him even more passionately as she felt him enter her. The initial waves of pain gave way to prolonged quivers of sheer ecstasy, until eventually Alistair rolled over and lay motionlessly beside her on the ground. Sarah cuddled into him and started kissing him again. As they lay there in the warmth of each other's embrace, they could hear the sound of someone whistling a tune in the distance. It startled them and brought them back to reality.

'Someone's coming, it must be Hamish,' said Sarah. 'I know a shortcut back to the house through the trees. Let's go. Quick!'

They had hardly reached the house before they heard the thud of Sneeshan's hooves again on the track.

'Glad you're here, Hamish,' Alistair said, his face flushed but his tone even. 'I was explaining to Sarah that I must now go directly to the prince and tell him about your success here.' As he mounted his horse, he glanced at Sarah. 'I will return as soon as I may, to see how you are faring.'

'He's off,' Hamish said as he watched him depart. 'What else did he say?'

'Not much,' said Sarah, reaching down to flick a piece of earth from her skirts, hoping to hide her blushes.

'I was hoping he had orders for me.'

'He didn't say anything … except about getting back to the prince and warning him about those soldiers heading for the Corrieyairack.' Sarah hoped her face did not betray her emotions.

She grabbed Hamish's outstretched hand and swung up behind him. It was habit that made her snuggle close and bring her arms around his waist, to hold on steady. It was not habit that brought his free hand to hers, pressing it to his chest. Sarah would have withdrawn her own hand, but it was comforting to have someone to hold on to, as little tears again began to prick her eyelids.

Hamish noticed that Sarah was very quiet, but put it down to the exhaustion of the day's events. Sarah indeed was very tired, and feeling very confused. The fire had been a success, but her day had been like no other so far in her short life. Two men had professed their love for her, and she had given her innocence to the one she truly loved.

CHAPTER 9

THERE WERE CHEERS OF welcome for the smoke-streaked pair as soon as they entered the croft. Dadda was grinning from ear to ear as he hugged Sarah, and planted a big wet whisky-laden kiss on her forehead. He grasped the exhausted Hamish firmly around the shoulders, and handed him his own bowl to drink from. The croft was filled with both tears of happiness and sadness. It didn't matter which. Bowls of ale flowed and Anghie retrieved another jug of whisky from its hiding place in the byre.

Returning from the peat bog, Jimmy had come across the remains of a young deer. It hadn't been fleet enough to outrun the flames, and lay charred on the blackened heather. Morag stayed to guard and gralloch the beast with a small knife, while Eileen and Jimmy ran and fetched a heather rope and a stout stick from Uncle Angus's whisky bothy. It wasn't long before the gutted animal was hanging by its bound legs from the pole, which the two girls proudly bore shoulder high down the hill.

While everyone was discussing the best way to cook or salt it, Ian Og and Angus turned up, and were surprised by all the merriment. Angus, the wily old miracle worker, then produced a precious onion from his sporran.

This was almost as much of a joy to Dadda as the day's events, and he carefully sliced it thinly. After taking a slice for himself, he offered it first to Grannie, then to the rest of the adults including Sarah, Hamish and Ian Og. It was the first time they had tasted onion, and everyone smiled as their eyes watered and they coughed.

While a proper bonfire was built outside to roast the venison in style, the fire in the hearth became the resting place for the large black pot. Barley and kale broth was warming within it, and Dadda cheerfully added a pair of hens that were owed to the laird for rent. 'Keppoch can wait until we have a couple more "Cain" hens.'

Neighbours began to drift over the hill to see what havoc the fire had wrought, and take a slice of venison. Women and old men stayed to share snuff or a pipe, and gather news of the war and their menfolk. The younger ones wanted to know of brave deeds and derring-do. The prince's gold button was reverently passed from hand to hand while Ian Og had to repeat his story again and again, until gradually he was too tired to talk any more.

As the night grew colder and rain began to dampen the bonfire, many drifted into the house while others made their way home. One by one the children crept to bed. Anghie and Sarah served the rest, listening to the tales, laughing at the old stories, and adding their own embellishments.

During the evening, Hamish tried to catch Sarah alone, but each time he did, there was another task that drew her away with a rueful smile. His head was dizzy with tiredness and his leg ached. Eventually he fell asleep at the table beside Ian Og, who was also asleep, still clutching the gold button in his bunched fist.

Looking at the two of them, Sarah felt like a load had been taken from her tired shoulders. Without Hamish's admiring eyes following her all the time, she was not so conscious now of her every move. Tomorrow would be another day and there would be time to speak with Hamish alone.

Sometime in the night, Angus drew her aside. 'What did Alistair say?' he asked quietly.

'Say ... when?' Sarah was somewhat startled as she had been thinking about Alistair.

'On the hill,' Angus looked intently at her. 'When you met him on the hill,' he emphasised.

'Say about what?' She felt herself redden, but hoped the gloom in the room would hide her blushes. Somehow, she thought that her uncle must have found out what had passed between Alistair and her.

'What he said about anything,' Angus was getting impatient.

'He didn't really say anything.'

'No message for me at all before he left?'

'Oh, that.' Her relief was palpable as she tried to think back to Alistair's parting words. 'No, nothing. Only that he was going to warn the prince.'

Angus was not so befuddled that he didn't notice her awkwardness. 'What do you mean "Oh, that"?' He was curious now. 'What else would he be talking about?'

'Nothing,' she spoke quietly but strongly. 'Nothing ... just the fire, and then he was gone.'

Her voice died altogether and she swallowed,

averting her eyes from a far too astute uncle's gaze. 'Dadda needs a drink.' She bustled away leaving Angus to ponder her words.

By first light the rain had stopped. Only the hardier members of the family remained gathered around the hearth inside, staring into the warm ashy remains of peat and log. Grannie was still there, smiling at the stories and talk of long-forgotten people. The excitement over, she was back in her twilight world, enjoying the banter and familiarity between the folk around her, and interjecting a meaningless comment now and again. The words of the three brothers prattled on like a stream, sometimes rushing, sometimes at a trickle. They wouldn't waste their precious moments at home on sleep.

Soon after sunrise, Ranald rinsed out one of the pots and set it on the blackened hearth with water for the porridge to sustain them all. He raked in some of the embers and added sticks and more peat to start building the fire again. Blue smoke hovered in a layer halfway up the room, as if waiting for permission to find its way to the raggedy hole in the roof. His brothers, Dadda and Roderick, began to stretch as the smoke shimmered and disappeared. It was the start of a new day.

Grannie set her own water in its little pot and added a pinch of tea before she took herself as usual to squat at the stream. From habit, Dadda and Roderick went out to look at the animals, although the cattle and sheep were still on the hill where the youngsters had driven them for safety. The movement from the house brought the dog to attention, distracted for the moment from hungrily eyeing the remaining hens scratching at the midden.

The two men strolled around to the shelter of the byre where Sneeshan and Pepper were standing quietly. Angel, the little Shetland pony, was also tethered there, and gave an unhappy whicker, being far from home and among strangers. Inside, Hamish and Ian Og were snuggled together in their plaids in the warm corner to which Angus had dragged them half-asleep sometime in the early hours. Now dead to the world, healing sleep was restoring the energy they'd been drained of over the past couple of days.

Angus himself had settled in the other corner, and when he saw the brothers, he rose and joined them while they walked the path to the old graveyard. At the lonely family cemetery, the three reverently knelt down on the damp ground beside the mounds. Roderick began to say the rosary aloud, while Angus and Dadda responded quietly with the familiar words.

In the croft, the young ones were not so keen to rise after such a late night, but the scent of Ranald's hot porridge seeped down into the depths of their dreamless sleep, and awoke the pangs of hunger that inevitably grips all healthy young bodies. In the glen, the comings and goings of fighting men was no longer a great novelty, but hunger was always a pressing concern.

The dull clatter of bowls being scraped clean and Grannie's bleat that a little honey would nourish her old bones were familiar sounds as the three men returned to the house.

It was Ranald who finally asked the unspoken question. 'Well? Are we going away today?'

Everyone looked at Dadda.

'Oh aye.' Despite the enthusiastic tone, Dadda suddenly took a great interest in a spot on the earthen floor. 'Yes. We'll have to get back ... I suppose.'

Roderick nodded resignedly, but brightened as a thought struck him. 'Mind you, we ought to gather in the beasts before we go.'

Dadda looked up, a grin beginning to widen his face, and he turned to Angus Sticks for approval. 'It wouldn't be right to just leave, would it? We've lost a lot of beasts with the weather this past couple of years, so we need to keep an eye on the rest. They'll be miles away in Kilcumin by tomorrow.'

'We wouldn't want that,' Angus agreed with a shake of his head and a smile on his face. 'Times are hard enough without the animals being scattered to the four winds.'

'Right!' said Dadda. 'We'll go this afternoon, once we've made sure the animals aren't astray.'

'But there's the peat, too,' said Roderick thoughtfully.

'Right enough,' Dadda nodded. 'Aye ... there's the peat too. It should be dry enough. And we have to check what kind of damage the fire has done.'

Everyone agreed.

Fresh from a couple of hours sleep, Sarah knew this was a golden opportunity and joined in. She looked out through the open door.

'The day's turning out well. It would be a pity to waste it. With three horses, we wouldn't take very long to bring in the peat that's up there.'

Anghie was quick to press home the point. 'Save a lot of trouble later, when the weather turns.'

'Oh, aye then,' said Dadda, his face now beaming. 'That's settled then. We'll leave tomorrow. Maybe we'll just have a dram now, to fortify us for the day.'

'Alistair might be back by then,' Angus added, as he poured a slug of whisky into Dadda's bowl and another in his own. 'He was to have instructions for us, so he'll probably make his way back here. He'd want us to wait for a day at least.' He looked at the pitcher in his hand. 'And it'll give me and Anghie a chance to sort out the bothy.'

The air of melancholy dispersed. Like the layer of peat smoke, it was gone as if it had never been there. It would be a busy day, but they were used to hard work and together it would be easier.

'Grannie and Sarah had better stay behind,' said Dadda. 'They're the ones we can spare.'

'I'm not staying here.' Grannie, as usual, wasn't going to miss any excitement.

'We could do with some food, Grannie. Maybe smoke the last of the venison,' Sarah cajoled, but the old woman wasn't to be distracted.

'I'm not staying here,' she said. 'And that's that.'

Nobody else wanted to stay behind either. Morag and Eileen pointed out that only they and Wee Jimmy knew where the animals were, and if they strayed over the hill they would be claimed by folk in the next glen.

Normally the animals would not be brought down from the hill until the weather grew bad in a couple of months' time, but with the soldiers nearby it would be prudent to bring them in a bit closer.

Angus and Anghie set off on Pepper towards the whisky bothy where precious barley and oats were hidden. It was decided that Roderick and the dog should go with Wee Jimmy and the twins, to gather up the animals out beyond the peat bog. It wasn't too far and they should return in good time to help with the peat.

Despite the bad headache that began to invade his whole body, Dadda led his troops out. The thirst in his mouth could have drained a loch. To outrun the hangover, he set off at a smart pace, matched only by a newly refreshed Ian Og, who led the Shetland pony piled high with wicker creels. Angel paid her creaking load almost no heed and walked happily between the two men.

Dadda was fascinated with Ian Og's minute creature and every few steps expressed his wonder. 'By Jove, that's an amazing animal!' Sometimes it was just 'Well, well!' and he would shake his head in disbelief. 'And it's such a wee pony.'

Then after a few paces, he said, 'and it took you from Keppoch to Blair Castle.'

'Aye, Dadda,' Ian Og tried to restrain his pride in the little mare.

A few steps further on. 'It wouldn't need much feeding either?'

'I don't know. She was hungry enough yesterday. But she belongs to John Cameron.' This conversation kept them going as they climbed the hill and Dadda began to feel better.

In the rear, Hamish led Sneeshan, with Grannie now sitting patiently atop, guarding some bannocks for the day's refreshment. In the past couple of days, a bond had sprung up between the two. Hamish joshed the old woman about being a great lady on a fine steed, and she was young again, flirting and calling him her ghillie.

Sarah was quiet as she walked with Hamish and Grannie. Hamish hoped her reticence could be put down to maidenly modesty, and he continued his banter with Grannie. Sarah wasn't listening, however. As they plodded up the trail, she tried to let the silly chat between the other two distract her from her worries.

All she could think about was Alistair, and these thoughts were making her feel uncomfortable. In case Hamish might try and read her mind, she said, 'I'd better keep up with the others. You and Grannie will be fine together.' Then she stepped ahead and maintained a measured tread that nearly, but never quite, caught up with Dadda and Ian Og. She strode onwards in a limbo of her own, with only a tangle of thoughts for company.

Up the hill, Dadda and Ian Og were relieved to find that the fire had swept across the hill away from the peat bog. The black lumps lay in neat rows waiting for collection. This was earlier than usual to collect them, but the sods were dry enough to be taken to the safety of the croft. The others began to arrive, and when Hamish and Grannie reached them, they were given the job of filling the creels. Neither was fit for any heavy work, and they seemed happy to keep each other company.

The horses were laden with the filled creels first, and then each person heaved one onto their own back and shoulder, before beginning the slow trek down the winding track. After Dadda's first enthusiastic rush, he settled to a steadier pace. It took some yards to adjust to the balance of a heavy creel, and caution was needed where the path was slippery. At the best of times, the track to the croft was rarely troublesome, but heavy loads made each journey longer than the last. It was a relief to reach the byre, and upend the basket on the growing fuel pile. A hasty drink of ale and a mouthful of bannock or cold venison refreshed each weary carrier before the return journey. A cheery word for whoever was coming down the track and soon enough it was time to offer one's back to Hamish for the next load.

Grime-streaked faces ran with sweat. Tired eyes reddened from fine dust and conversation grew sparse.

Hamish offered cheery words as he helped lift full baskets onto tired animals and backs. Grannie had a soothing salve for skinned hands, but Sarah wasn't the only one who found it harder and harder to raise a smile each time she returned to the peat bog. Her energies were spent on the relentless climbing, up and down.

The arrival of Roderick, the twins and Wee Jimmy with the sheep and goats gave them all fresh heart. The three youngsters were told to herd the animals further down the glen, and when they finished they went to stack the peat where it might have a better chance of drying well at the croft, while Roderick joined the straggling line of carriers.

By the time the twins and Wee Jimmy arrived back at the house, the sods of peat were beginning to spill over quite a large area. Stacking it neatly would offer protection against rain. The three were tired but diligently gathered all the stray sods closer together, and a black wall began to rise against the end of the byre.

The next time Sarah tipped out her basket and took a breather, she was heartened to see how high the mound had progressed. As the twins and Wee Jimmy stacked their last load, drizzle began to fall again. It was a welcome relief after a hot sweaty day's work. Everyone was given a bowl of ale or a dram of whisky and slowly their spirits revived.

As he led Sneeshan towards the croft, Hamish was limping quite noticeably, but he steadied himself from time to time with a reassuring hand on the horse's neck. Angel, the little Shetland pony, had also proved a willing worker and Ian Og led her to rest in the byre.

Bent double under her final creel of turf, Sarah picked her way down the path, and marvelled at the wiry strength within Grannie Morag, who was several yards in front of her. The old woman, who looked as if a breath of wind would knock her over, had packed and hauled creels for Hamish all day, and then insisted in bearing a load herself on the final journey. Although it was the smallest creel and only half-full, it looked nearly as large as herself. She moved forward rhythmically and sure-footed down the old path, muttering her prayers at each step.

Angus and Anghie joined them at the house as the last lump of peat was tucked into the stack. A sigh of relief from all rose up through the fine rain. There was an air of festivity not yet dampened by thoughts of parting in the morning. Cheerful company made the chicken broth, venison and potatoes seem like a feast. If sometimes the gaiety was a little forced, no one minded. Thirst further improved Sarah's barley beer, and the latest sample of Angus's whisky was downed enthusiastically. The batch begun today would be made by Anghie, now the assistant distiller, as Alistair and Ian Og had been before him.

It was Grannie who made the first move to bed. She had eaten and drunk heartily. The younger children were glad to follow her lead and leave Sarah with the menfolk. She was also dog-tired and would have laid her bedding out in the wee room with the others, but there were chores to be seen to. Most would wait till the morrow, but Hamish's leg needed checking. Uncle Ranald was the other healer in the family, and together he and Sarah unwound the bandage and lifted off the mush that lay beneath. Both were happy that the day's work seemed to have had no adverse effect, so they laid more leaves on the wound and rebound the leg.

As Sarah held his leg steady, Hamish kept smiling at her, and there was no mistaking the warmth of his feelings as he squeezed her hand. Thinking it might be a good time to leave him to his own thoughts, Sarah went out to check on the dog and chickens.

After a few moments Hamish stood up and said he would go outside and stretch his legs before turning in for the night. The interaction between the two had not gone unnoticed. Dadda and the uncles exchanged knowing smiles.

Out in the twilight Hamish was less circumspect. In a moment, he took hold of Sarah's wrist and drew her into the shelter of the byre. She was clasped within his arms for a moment, until a discreet cough from the back door and her name being called out brought her back to her senses. When she returned to the croft she could see big grins hastily disappearing off the men's faces, but she tried to remain nonchalant while she took her bedding through to the other room, leaving them to their own chatter.

The next morning, it was the sound of movement in the big room that woke Sarah. She rose immediately and chivvied at the youngsters to start the day. Ranald's porridge was bubbling on the newly stoked fire. Anghie was bringing in fuel and making room for a family breakfast together before the travellers took their leave. Once again, Dadda, Roderick and Angus went out to the little graveyard to say farewell. On their way back they woke the two younger men in the byre. It would soon be time to gather up swords and muskets, and return to the service of the prince.

The five of them were laughing loudly when they returned to the croft. Adventure beckoned them in different directions, and although Sarah did not hear the words, she knew by his blush and sheepish grin that Hamish was being teased again. They were all in good humour.

'Come on now. Breakfast is ready for the travellers.'

Dadda sat down with a flourish. 'A sup of ale to wet the whistle and a dram to fortify us,' he said as he poured.

The others arranged themselves around the table. The younger ones served their elders while conversation flowed between them all. There were instructions from Dadda to the girls, and cautions from Sarah to Hamish about his leg. Angus gave directions about distilling to Anghie, and Ian Og teased the twins and Wee Jimmy.

Sarah always enjoyed this family banter, so it was a few minutes before she realised that Grannie was missing. Even as she went quietly through to the other room, a strange sensation told her something was wrong. No illness or discomfort would have prevented the old lady from taking her place at the table. Even before she entered the room, she knew.

Returning to the family, her tears began to flow as she said, 'Grannie's dead! It must have been sometime during the night.'

The last of her words were lost in a hubbub of voices, followed by a hushed stillness. Ranald was the first to move. He rushed to verify that his mother was truly dead. There was still some warmth in the body, but the waxy mask of death was already on her face. Ranald laid her straight and crossed her hands upon her chest.

He spoke to her as one would a small child. 'I'm just straightening you, Mamma.'

It was almost in case he might be hurting her. She looked peaceful. The rest of the preparations could take place after the family had filed in to say goodbye.

CHAPTER 10

THERE COULD BE NO thought of anyone leaving now. Morag MacDonell had lived her life faithfully to the very end, and was entitled to full and proper ritual, before crossing over into the hands of God and her ancestors. In normal times, Father Malachy at Roy Bridge would have been the first person to be called upon, but he had gone with the clansmen to serve the prince, as had many other priests. Two women were the first to arrive after Ian Og rode down the glen with the news. The door was open in expectation of their arrival and they entered with bowed heads, only briefly nodding to the three chief mourners sitting in the main room quietly reciting the rosary, so loved by Grannie.

The women went into the wee room and the door was closed. A moment or two later Sarah came out and beckoned young Morag and Eileen to join them. Furniture was moved, and the girls brought out everything that would not be required. There were muted sounds of talk and prayer. They fetched and carried quietly, heads bowed solemnly until finally the women emerged. Their work done, Ranald, the eldest son, saw them out of the house, and pressed a coin into each hand as he shook it on their departure.

In the middle of the wee room Grannie lay peacefully upon her bed. A brass candlestick, which must have been brought by one of the women, bore a fine wax candle, made no doubt by Grannie herself with the help of the bees, and stored for this occasion. It cast a warm gentle light upon the shrunken form, now dressed in a linen plaid and looking as if she was resting. Clasped in her hands was her rosary, a comfort both in life and death. The lower part of her body was draped with a coverlet strewn with bog myrtle and yew, which softly scented the air.

Dadda dearly wanted Grannie to be buried in a wooden coffin, but the young joiner from Glen Roy had gone with the prince. His father, although he could no longer see, allowed Ian Og and Hamish to take eight precious nails and enough wood to decently house the old lady on her last journey.

As Roderick and his two apprentices began to assemble the simple box, Ranald went up to the hives. For most of her life, Grannie would visit the bees and tell them all the news of the family, but for many years now Ranald had taken on the task. He stood between the two hives for a few minutes watching insects flying in and out, and then spoke to them of his mother's death. Tears fogged his vision, but he told of her bravery with the soldiers and her work with the peat yesterday, and how he would miss her. The bees hovered for a moment and then took the news with them out across the moorland.

It was fortunate that the weather had cleared up. The women and girls of the family gathered together preparing food, while Angus Sticks and Anghie took Wee Jimmy out from under their feet, and went to check on the whisky, cattle and sheep.

Dadda's brother-in-law, Uncle Angus, who in his stride could face and rout a dozen hardy men, was trying to put a brave face on his own sadness. He was sorely affected by Grannie's death. She'd treated him like one of her own sons, scolding and praising in equal measure, and loving him wholeheartedly. He didn't feel he had quite the same right to grief as the three brothers, but he was weighed down with sadness. He hoped a day out on the hill with Angie and Wee Jimmy would give him time to let the loss sink in.

Dadda was supposed to check on the beasts closer to the house, but mostly he sat looking into the fire and sighing. The quiet mumble of prayers being recited in the other room was only interrupted when more visitors came to pay their respects to the deceased, and offer their condolences to the living.

For refreshments, there was whisky and ale to drink, and brandy offered to some more notable visitors. Sweet cakes with honey and dried fruit hoarded for special occasions like this were also served. Some might take a morsel and then transfer the treasure to a pocket or sporran for later. Tobacco and snuff were particular favourites with many of the women. The sizzle of brown spit hitting the fire punctuated the conversation.

Each visit began with quiet chatter and fond memories of Grannie. There were few left who could remember her as a young woman, but each cup and bowl that was filled and refilled awakened recollections, and old stories and wry laughter were shared.

Reverently, on Sunday, the third day, Roderick brought the assembled coffin to the wee room and the old lady was lifted into it. Although many of the local men were on the prince's trail, a good number had come home to plant vital crops for next year, and had gathered both inside and outside the house to honour Grannie Morag. Ranald raised his voice so that as many of the gathering as possible might hear him, reading out prayers commending his mother into God's care.

There was silence for a few moments while the lid of the makeshift coffin was carefully laid down, and Grannie was lost to sight. Sarah felt it was the loneliest moment she could ever remember. The box was reverently manhandled through both doors and into the breezy morning air. Tears that remained unshed began to flow. In front of the croft the mourners were assembled, and by the time the sun was high, the cortège was ready to move.

Like most of the warriors, Ranald of the Rock, the usual piper at local funerals, was with the prince, but his thirteen-year-old son, with his own pipes suitably draped in black streamers, led the procession, playing the Glen Rowan lament.

Grannie's three sons and Ian Og, her eldest grandson, followed, bearing the coffin waist-high on ropes they held between them. Anghie and Wee Jimmy solemnly marched beside them, each holding a token end of rope. The sorely depleted company of men, led by Hamish, stepped in behind them.

Sarah, Morag and Eileen stood at the door with the rest of the women, and tearfully watched them disappear up the track, before going to clear the small room where Grannie had lain. While the bed was stripped, Sarah took the yew and myrtle and threw it on the fire where it crackled and sparked, giving off a fine perfume. She made the sign of the cross with one large sprig, to clear the air of any spirits that might be lingering where Grannie had been resting.

At the old graveyard there wasn't enough room for all the men to gather within its low walls, and most arrayed themselves outside, creating a welcome windbreak. The tearful mourners watched as Angus and her three sons solemnly lifted Grannie Morag from the makeshift coffin into her final resting place. This time it was Roderick, who led the prayers, committing his mother to the earth where her husband should have been lying for the past thirty years, but he had died in battle and his body never recovered.

When the mound received its final pats with the back of a spade, it was the signal for old cousin Roddy to deliver a eulogy. He was one of the few that remembered Grannie Morag as the bonny wee lass and healer who became a faithful wife, loving mother and kind grandmother, even though she could be a little autocratic in her ways. He remembered her laughter and her tears, and knew that with her mind restored in the Great Beyond, God would find her a worthy and entertaining companion.

Old Roddy did not spend too long on his words. The cold winds discouraged verbosity. There were shivers of relief when he finished, and general chat broke out as the company began to withdraw from the graveyard. Surreptitiously, a few mourners gathered up some of the newly dug earth on the grave, and carefully tied it in a corner of their plaid. Being from the grave of a healer, it would have restorative properties.

With a handshake or a word for family members, the mourners walked back down the path. Duty done, many returned to the croft to speak to the girls and collect their women, and then carried along the path towards their own homes, little groups keeping each other company over the hill. The rest took up the invitation to partake of more refreshment before they too made their departure.

As the men of the family returned to the house, the chatter could be heard several yards away. It was hardly correct to call the visitors 'guests'. All were related to each other. The occasion was a mixture of sadness at the recent bereavement, and cheer at getting together. They were satisfied that the funeral had been fitting. Old Roddy was mightily praised for his words, and repeated them several times when asked to do so by different women.

Ian Og was more interested in old Roddy's daughter Jane, who was turning into a dimple-cheeked beauty with an engaging smile. Without the young men of the clan, he had little competition and was not one to miss such a fine opportunity. Although he dutifully spoke to the older visitors, ensuring that they were plied with food and drink, he made especially sure that Jane was offered the tastiest sweetmeats and the best brandy.

The younger members of the family appeared to accept the death of Grannie Morag much more pragmatically than their elders. Wee Jimmy was engrossed in the diversions it brought: cousins to meet and play with. Eileen and Morag had felt very grown up being included with the women when Grannie had been laid out, but now they had friends to mingle with. Some they hadn't seen for a long time, because they lived too far away for regular meetings. It was an occasion to fit faces with names. Many they'd heard about only occasionally around the fire at night.

The assembly was taking care of itself. There was nothing more to be done and Sarah went to inspect the little room where Grannie had always slept. The old bits and pieces were back in place, and she sat on Grannie's bed. Some beeswax on the ground showed where the candlestick had been.

Hamish appeared in the doorway. He carried a brimming bowl of ale and offered it to her. She was thirsty and drank it down with relish before returning the bowl.

'How are you doing?' he asked.

'I'm fine now,' she smiled. 'I'm just tired.'

'You've worked hard.' He leaned forward and kissed her gently on the mouth.

'Hamish! There are people watching,' she protested.

'No one's watching. They're all next door.'

'But if they saw us ...'

'They wouldn't take a bit of notice.' And he kissed her again to emphasise the point. It wasn't a passionate meeting of lips, rather the caress of a loving friend.

Shortly afterwards, when Dadda passed the doorway and looked in, he smiled when he saw the two heads close to each other talking very quietly.

'You know I'll have to go with Angus, maybe tomorrow,' Hamish said.

'You've been very good, Hamish. I know you didn't mean to stay so long. It's meant a lot to me.'

'Has it really?' He took her hand.

'Oh yes.' Slowly she withdrew her hand. 'I don't know what I'd have done without you.'

Sarah continued. 'Uncle Angus was a great help too. He was very good with the younger ones and you were wonderful to go with Ian Og to fetch the wood and help Uncle Roderick. Dadda would have been so upset if we'd not had a coffin,' she babbled. 'And your leg not fully better yet.'

Hamish's face fell. 'Was it just because I was useful?' He studied her carefully. 'Was there not another reason?'

'Oh, I can't think like that now, Hamish.'

'But you do care for me, don't you?'

'Of course I do.' As if to show how true it was, she leaned forward and kissed him softly on the mouth before standing up, taking a deep breath and going to join the others.

The afternoon and evening passed. There was music and storytelling into the night, and more than once it was said that Grannie herself would have enjoyed the ceilidh.

Gradually, the company began to thin as other duties pressed and friends left. Several men could easily have been persuaded to stay on for a second day to keep the family company, but gradually everyone took their leave. Sarah was grateful that the prince had taken most of the clan away. Had all the cousins been in the district, the house would not have emptied for at least a week. She knew she couldn't cope with that just now.

When the last mourner finally left, it became obvious that all three brothers were taking their mother's death very hard. Dadda and Roderick found solace in the brandy and strong whisky, but Ranald grew very quiet. Only the bees witnessed his tears, but his red eyes and nose told their own story. Angus had borne his sadness without much outward show, but now that the responsibilities of the funeral were over, he took himself to the byre. Pepper, Sneeshan and Angel stood quietly, as he as he tearfully drank until the alcohol softened the edges of his sorrow.

CHAPTER 11

SARAH WAS TIRED AND melancholy going to bed in the little room that night. The twins were soon settled together in Grannie's bed. Wee Jimmy was fast asleep in his usual place on the straw in the corner. Sarah lay quietly in the girls' smaller bed but could get little sleep, as she listened to the restless little grunts of the others, while her mind was taken up with the funeral and Grannie.

When daylight eventually seeped into the room, her whole body still felt crushed with tiredness. There was dampness on her skin, which meant there would be rain soon. Only habit made her force her weary bones to start the day. Everyone else lacked enthusiasm too. There was no cheery banter at the table, while Ranald's porridge was eaten, but without any obvious enthusiasm. Usually the day's work would be discussed, but not on this grey morning.

Hamish, Ian Og and Anghie were already up and gone out. When they found themselves awake so early, they went hunting with the dog on the moor. They knew that Angus would be in no fit state to depart for a while.

Sarah was left with a sorry bunch of long faces. Wee Jimmy began to moan and complain that the others had promised to take him hunting but had left without him. In desperation, she sent him to catch fish in the burn. 'And don't come back without something,' she warned as he plodded out of the room.

'It's not fair! Why do I have to do it?' he muttered as he left. Soon enough, he was busily following the track of a wild cat, all thought of fish forgotten.

The girls couldn't be persuaded to settle down at the carding and spinning, which had fallen behind, and they opted instead to check on the two calves that were out with the cattle. Sarah was too tired to argue.

Nor was it likely that the men would be prodded into activity. Angus was still dead to the world in the shelter of the byre. Roderick and Ranald rose from the table as soon as they had eaten, forestalling any orders by saying they were going down to the graveyard and might check on the sheep. When Dadda finally awoke, Sarah asked him about the animals. He only shook his head and sighed, 'Ah pet,' as he went off to walk down the glen.

By herself, Sarah found the house very empty. Outside, there were spirits in the air: souls of the dead borne on the wind to escort new brethren. She hadn't the heart to go and collect some kale. Instead, with a sprig of elder tucked in her hair to ward off any evil, she fetched water for the pot and peat for the fire. There were no eggs to be found. The hens had obviously been upset by the presence of the departed and were not laying today.

Beside the fire, Sarah settled down and mindlessly began to brush the card combs against each other, deftly turning out roll upon roll of soft wool onto a growing pile. She dearly missed the constant mumbles and grumbles of Grannie Morag. The spinning wheel stood silently on the other side of the hearth. As she worked, Sarah began to see an elusive image of her own mother sitting behind it, foot rocking steadily, back and forth, back and forth, feeding the soft rolls into a never-ending thread. She could even hear the faint *'whirr.... whirr'* as it went around and around. Mamma looked at her and gave a gentle smile, but her face was tired and sad as the wheel turned and turned.

'Mamma,' whispered Sarah, unsure of the meaning of this vision. 'What's wrong?' The shady image gently shook its head, and continued to feed wool into the spindle. Slowly it faded like mist in the morning sunshine.

It was the distant bark of the dog that recalled Sarah to the living. The carding battens were still poised in her hands as she stood up, trying to clear her head and think of what was to be done. The family would all be returning hungry, looking for broth and bannocks.

Lifting the lid of the big pot, it was not surprising to find there was barely enough mutton left to make a modest dinner for even a single member of the household. She could only hope that the hunters might have found a deer, a fat hare or a couple of grouse to stretch the meat. If not, at least there would be barley and oatmeal to fill the void.

When she went out to the storage bothy and opened the little door, Sarah's heart nearly stopped. The place was almost bare. She knew the funeral might deplete it of honey and exotic rarities like dried fruit, but thought there would still be enough dried meat and fish to tide them over.

The many visitors had also taken a toll on barley and oatmeal stocks, and with no hens laying eggs, Keppoch was in danger of getting no rent at all this year. A terrible feeling washed over her and stark images invaded her mind. Winter was not far off. All the stored food was gone and there would be nothing to eat. She pictured Anghie and the younger children wasting away, one by one getting thinner, little bundles joining Grannie. It was these images that became too much for her. The dam burst, her knees buckled and she dropped to the earthen floor of the bothy. Great racking sobs shook her whole body and tears flooded from her eyes.

The dog, returning from the mountain ahead of the men, was the first to investigate the strange sounds. He sniffed at the inert, noisy Sarah, and then gave way to the humans who followed. When she looked up and saw Hamish, Anghie and Ian Og, the torrent of tears flowed even faster.

'What is it? What is it?' Hamish bent down, shocked by this great emotion.

'Mamma ...' she wailed. 'Spinning ... I saw her ...'

Hamish was confused by the words and couldn't guess what they meant. He clasped her close, patting her head. 'There there ... my dearest ... Sshh now.'

Sarah's words kept coming out, a senseless stream, all mixed up.

'There. There ... sshh ...' He rocked her gently.

Everyone had chosen this time to return to the croft. The girls saw the group and came over. Roderick and Ranald arrived from checking the sheep. Dadda came up the track with Wee Jimmy, who was proudly bearing a trout. They were all mystified.

'What's going on?' Dadda kept asking of nobody in particular. 'What's wrong?'

The last one to join the group was a very white-faced Angus. Taking a look over everyone's shoulders, he pulled the onlookers away. 'Come on now, leave them in peace.'

He shepherded them all into the croft. 'She'll be fine.' He spoke quietly and carefully. 'I'm sure of it. We'll maybe get a pot onto the fire and make her some broth.'

Dadda and the uncles took their cue from him, and set the girls at spinning and sent Wee Jimmy to fetch kale. Angus poured out a large measure of brandy, draining it himself before refilling the cup and taking it out to the bothy. 'Here,' he said, handing it to Hamish, who was almost crooning to the stricken, sobbing Sarah. Angus turned and went back down to the croft.

'Take some of this, my dove.' Hamish held the cup to her lips and although she made a face, he smiled encouragingly.

'Yes. Go on. That's it.'

Whilst everyone was sitting in the croft discussing the phenomenon of Sarah's distraction, she reluctantly sipped Angus's brandy. Gradually, her words began to make sense and Hamish heard her fears about winter, and looking after the younger children without any food.

'They say the fighting will be over by Christmas, but what if it's not?' she sobbed. 'We'll be all on our own with nothing to eat.' The words ended in a wail.

'Oh, Sarah,' Hamish was nearly crying now at her distress. 'Oh no, it'll be all right. You'll see. I'll make sure you're all right.'

Angus returned with Dadda and more of the whisky. 'What's the matter?' He asked.

Hamish had by now pieced together most of what Sarah was trying to say. He looked up at them both. 'She's worried about the winter and food.'

'Is that all, lassie?' Dadda crouched at the door of the bothy. 'Don't you worry ... we'll all make sure there's food for the winter.'

'I told her that,' Hamish said in a consoling manner. 'I said we'd all look after the family.'

'Och aye,' Angus grinned from ear to ear. 'I can always find meal for whisky and you never know,' he paused for dramatic effect, 'I might just let you have a morsel or two.'

The truth of this brought a wry smile to Sarah's lips and she nodded.

'So you'll dry your eyes and not be thinking daft thoughts?'

'No,' she sniffed purposefully.

'And we never died a winter yet, did we?' Angus smiled at her.

She shook her head in agreement. 'No.'

'Good girl,' he said.

Reassured, he took the empty cup and was about to drag Dadda away, when Sarah's face clouded again.

'Mamma was here,' she said. 'She came to warn me.'

'Mamma ... was here?' Dadda repeated.

'Our Mary?' said Angus at the same time.

'Yes.'

Dadda leaned forward anxiously. 'What did she say?'

'She didn't say anything.'

'Well, what did she do?'

'Nothing really, she was at the spinning wheel. You know the way she was. But she looked so sad.'

'Sad?' All three men spoke the word.

'Yes.' Her voice was almost a whisper, and little tears began to escape again.

'But she didn't say anything?' Angus asked again.

'No. Nothing'

'Are you sure it was a warning? Maybe she just wanted to see you.'

'I don't know.'

'Maybe she was just sorry that you were so unhappy,' Dadda suggested.

Sarah pondered this for a moment. 'I don't think so.'

'But you are unhappy,' he pointed out. 'What with Grannie dying like that.'

'I suppose so.'

'So it'll be all right.' Hamish gave her a gentle squeeze. 'You'll see. Your Mamma would never bring bad news, would she?'

'No. I suppose not.' Sarah was reluctantly allowing herself to be convinced. 'But ...'

'We'll be fine over the winter. Nobody will starve.' Angus spoke determinedly.

'And there's family down the glen.' Dadda took the same firm tone. It was the sound of reason, and although the black tide of sadness didn't completely disappear, the kindness of the three men reminded Sarah that she wasn't on her own, whatever might happen.

She nodded and tried to raise a little smile. 'Yes, of course ... I know.' Tears still tumbled down her cheeks. 'But Mamma looked so sad,' she added, as she sniffed and drew the back of her hand across her nose.

The three men waited with encouraging words until she was composed, and then led her back into the croft. Hamish held her hand and gave it a squeeze before letting go. The rest of the family looked to see if there would be any further outbursts, and when she smiled tentatively there was a general sigh of relief.

Two days later the family were gathered under the early morning autumn clouds outside the wee house, to bid farewell to the warriors. The wind breezed lightly against their clothing, but it looked to be a good day.

'Bring us back something nice, Dadda.'

'We'll have to do that,' he agreed, as he caressed each child: a stroke on a cheek, a pat on the head.

Behind the bright glitter in his eyes, Dadda's thoughts were black. Although everyone acted as if it were forgotten, Sarah's outburst weighed heavily on his mind. It was her vision which troubled him most.

Why would his dead wife appear to his daughter? It was true the clan were heading out to battle, but death on the battlefield following his chief was an honourable end for any highlander, and shouldn't occasion portents. And if it did, she should have visited him.

'Oh Mary,' he thought. 'Just to see your face again, I would walk through the fires of hell itself.'

He blinked to ward off the tears threatening to rise in his eyes.

Despite his assurances to the contrary, there was a real danger of hunger in the glen. Like the rain, it was never very far away, but they always managed somehow to feed everyone and he hoped this year they would too, despite the absence of the men.

With a wan smile of affection, he clasped Sarah close. 'You're a grand girl. You'll make that lad a good wife.' It was said quietly in her ear. She couldn't see his face, but knew Dadda meant Hamish, who stood nearby. 'Aw! Dadda!' she tried to admonish him. 'Don't be talking like that. Not now.'

'Not now?' Dadda was not to be put off. 'Now's the very time.' His hand engulfed hers and he patted it warmly, before he drew Hamish beside him with a wide beckoning gesture, and clasped their two hands together in an unmistakable gesture of betrothal. It was a sign of his approval in the face of promised battles ahead, as sentimental tears began to course down his cheeks.

Sarah's awkward smile was most becoming and a red glow began to colour her neck and suffuse her face. Hamish beamed at her blushes. His own radiance vied with his red hair and almost outshone the sun, which suddenly broke through the clouds as he leaned over and kissed her joyfully.

'We'll have to have a dram on that before we leave,' said Dadda, cheerfully herding everyone back inside.

During the little celebration that followed, Angus took Sarah to one side. 'Are you happy, my pet?'

Her smile was perhaps a little too tight as she nodded, and Angus knew something was not quite right. He did not know what it was but he knew it somehow involved Alistair. I'm glad for you,' he continued. 'Hamish is a good man. He's both brave and kind.'

Again her lips widened and her cheeks dimpled. She was close to confessing her confusion and concern to her mother's brother. She hesitated and the moment passed, but until he left she could feel Angus watching her thoughtfully from time to time.

The sun had long since chased away the last of the clouds before the 'deoch an dorus' was finally downed, and everyone gathered again at the edge of the track. This time they kept their farewells brief.

'Time we were away,' said Roderick, before Dadda could find another excuse to return to the shelter of the house.

Ranald, Roderick and Dadda turned for the blackened track over the mountains to Blair and Perth where the prince was heading. Dadda's ready tears spilled over again, but he stepped out as lively as his brothers, and once home was out of sight, the mighty challenges ahead beckoned him like good ale did a thirsty man.

Several days later, Angus was talking to Hamish and Ian Og. 'It's been over a week, and no word from Alistair. He was to give me instructions, but I think we'll serve him best back at Ardgour and the Corran Narrows.'

Ian Og first had to return the pony, Angel, to Keppoch and Margaret Cameron, who would be unaware that her man did not have it. On his way he could learn what news there was and bring any messages. 'I'll meet you at Ardgour in a few days,' he called over his shoulder, as the little beast stepped out along the westward trail.

Now only Angus and Hamish were left. While Sarah and the youngsters watched, the big man gathered his weapons and bade farewell to each in turn. Hugs and kisses and handshakes were meted out according to the recipient. Then there was just Sarah. As he hugged her he bent his head and said quietly, 'You'd tell me, wouldn't you, if there was anything troubling you?'

She sighed and lied, 'Yes, Uncle Angus. Of course I would.'

They all waved as he set off down the glen, his horse loaded with several flagons of whisky. Hamish was to follow on Sneeshan with the bulk of the load. They were heading back to Maryburgh to sell some whisky, and Hamish wanted to reassure his anxious mother, and keep an eye on the comings and goings of the soldiers there.

When Angus was finally out of sight, Hamish and Sarah were still standing together outside the croft. Anghie tried to distract the other children with chores, but they kept peeping at the two standing awkwardly together.

Laughing, Hamish drew Sarah around to the byre where the spectators couldn't gawp at them, and once inside he shut the door. Gently his arms enfolded her. He kissed her softly, his tongue gently brushing her ear and nose before seeking the warmth of her mouth.

For Sarah, this brought a tumult of emotions from within. Despite initial reticence, she was becoming aroused by Hamish. At the same time she remembered Grannie's comments about taking care of herself. If she was truly betrothed to Hamish, he would not wish to know that Alistair still held a special place in her heart. To deceive him would be a kindness, especially as there had been no word from Alistair, and no approach to Dadda either. The caresses became more urgent, and when Hamish laid her gently down in the straw, she succumbed to his love-making and finally lay at peace with his arms around her.

'It's hard to leave you now, my love,' he whispered, reluctantly drawing away. Taking her hand, he kissed her fingertips and stood up. 'Dearest Sarah, I must go. I have to be on the prince's business.'

For Sarah, the words were both beautiful and hard to bear. She loved this gentle strong friend, but deep down she knew it was Alistair she truly loved, down to the roots of her being. What happened with Hamish would have been the sweetest moment in the world, except that she still could not erase images of Alistair from her mind.

CHAPTER 12

As PEPPER AMBLED DOWN the track towards Maryburgh and Fort William, Angus's thoughts were of Sarah's vision. What was its meaning? Why would his sister Mary appear at this time?

During the past days, the whole family had worked heroically together and prevented a tragedy at the hands of the soldiers. Grannie Morag had played a major part in their defeat. She'd led a good life caring for her family and it ended with a great triumph. Travelling into the next world would not be a hardship for her, though it brought a black void to those left behind who loved her. Angus would greatly miss her kindness and bracing love, but it was Sarah's vision of Mamma, his own dear sister Mary, which now kept floating into his mind.

Angus had noticed that Sarah was also very affected by the vision of her mother, but she didn't say why. Maybe she just didn't know. Was the message for her alone, and what might it be? Her betrothal to Hamish cheered the whole family. Clearly, Hamish was a good man who loved Sarah dearly, but Angus still had a niggling feeling that something wasn't quite right. Was Hamish, indeed, the right man for Sarah?

His mind kept churning on the mystery. Why his sister would come to warn the Jacobite warriors puzzled him. He had heard from clan members that the prince and his followers were already down in England It seemed their action was gaining momentum and, for God-fearing men, it was their sworn duty to support the anointed king and his son, Charles Stuart, to gain the crown. He dismissed the idea that she might be warning anyone against that. The Lochaber clans had no doubts about their allegiance, and that their duty lay with the cause, to crown Charles as God's rightful king.

By the time Angus reached Maryburgh, a rather subdued Hamish had caught up with him. The conversation between them was mostly of practical matters, and Angus tactfully avoided asking any teasing questions about Sarah or the family. He did, however, mention Sarah's vision, but it made no sense to Hamish either.

The town before them was quiet. Jacobite rumblings were affecting the whole district and folk were waiting to see what would happen. Pot shots to and from the fort were common, so they took a sheltered, muddy path between the houses.

As they made their way, Angus said, 'I am heading for Inverness, but first I must go to see how my brother and sisters are faring in Strathnairn. I'm not sure how long I might be there, but tell Anghie to start the next batch of whisky whenever the grain arrives.'

When they reached the alehouse, it too seemed quiet, but the cheerful innkeeper welcomed the delivery as the drizzle continued. 'Good timing, Angus,' he said as they both brought a load into the shed. 'They'll all come, Jacobite or Hanoverian, whether to rejoice or mourn.'

'Aye,' said Angus. 'There's plenty here for them and I'll bring more, whenever I get the chance.'

Having made their delivery, the two riders bowed their heads against the mizzling rain and, in that companionable silence born of long acquaintanceship, made their way to Hamish's house. His mother Lizzie came to see who was at the door. 'Come in, come in,' she said when she saw them. As they entered Angus felt that Lizzie was less frigid than he remembered. He was surprised to be invited inside to shelter from the weather. Normally, he would have declined and turned away, but she was from Inverness, not far from Strathnairn where his own family came from. He was happy to enter the house and hear any news she might have.

While they gossiped about family and friends in Dornoch, Strathnairn and Inverness, Lizzie spoke of Jacobite hopes that French supporters and supplies would be arriving soon. The Hanoverian loyalists were doing all they could to stop any landings. As she spoke, he got the impression that this information came from a reliable source. She seemed very well informed.

When Hamish had settled his horse for the night out of the cold wind, he joined them.

'It's an awful night for travelling, Angus,' he said. 'Perhaps you should stay and rest for a while?'

'Thanks, Hamish, but I am well used to travelling in the rain and I don't want to outstay my welcome here with your good mother.'

'Angus, you're welcome to stay the night and I can make up a wee bed for you.'

'Thanks, Lizzie! No, I'll be on my way. I have delayed

long enough. I wish you both well for the winter and the difficult months that lie ahead.'

Angus took his leave and was again surprised when Lizzie said, 'Goodbye Angus, call in any time.' At the door he shook Hamish's hand in farewell, then led the patient Pepper between the wee houses and headed towards the grey stone fort, a forbidding sullen shadow in the gathering dark, overlooking Loch Linnhe.

Close to the great wooden gates, watchmen were on duty. They knew Angus well and asked no questions. Without words, one of the men went to fetch the quartermaster, a decent down-to-earth man. When he wanted whisky, he dealt quietly with Angus, and each could be relied upon to keep his mouth shut. If their trade was officially observed, consequences for both could be dire.

It wasn't long before the wicket gate opened. Angus urged the packhorse to enter and a few minutes later emerged with empty whisky flagons and welcome siller tucked into his sporran. Without haste, the pony made her way through the town before turning towards Inverness. They travelled along Wade's great military road for a while, and then to avoid any soldiers, he turned onto the old Highland trail along the Great Glen.

Angus kicked Pepper into a gentle trot and headed towards Inverness. It was a dreich night, and although it was only October, there was snow on top of the hills. Angus knew the track well so both man and animal were content to keep up a steady pace. It had been a profitable day, but Sarah's vision still pressed heavily on his mind. He was growing more and more concerned that the warning from his dead sister concerned him, and there was only one way to find out.

By nightfall, the rain had eased and the rising moon helped light his path towards the family home. It lay beside the old road that ran from Inverness to Strathnairn. Visitors had always been welcomed as were the news and gossip they brought. After his parents died, Angus, being the eldest, went to work on a neighbouring estate to earn some badly needed money. His younger brother, Roddy, and his sisters, Jean and Rosie, were left to till their small bit of land and look after the one milk cow.

Over the past year, the had rising curtailed Angus's visits, but now his heart warmed at the thought of seeing his childhood home and the flickering light from two wee windows. Turning the last bend of the hill, he stopped short. His heart began beating wildly and he wondered what horrors he was likely to find. Only a few yards ahead, the croft lay derelict and in darkness. Much of the roof was collapsed and the door gone. He drew Pepper around to the back, hidden from any watchers, and hitched her to an overhanging branch. Taking a deep breath to steady himself, he cautiously began making his way inside, not knowing what he might find.

With a tinderbox from his sporran, he set a spark on some straw. This gave light enough to find and kindle a dry stick to lie in the hearth and start a fire. He found a suet candle and when it was lit, it showed the damage that had been wrought. Peat ash was scattered over the floor and walls. The table was broken, a chair and a platter or two lay in pieces, and there was a rainy puddle at one end. Looking around outside in the fading light, there were no human remains, nor tell-tale bloodstains. He found no bloody clothing or bedding, so he knew the family must have escaped before the croft had been ransacked.

He wedged some table planks up against the broken front door. When he felt all was secure, Angus brought in his pack and laid it beside the now-glowing fire. Gathering fragments of peat and bits of wood that were strewn around the floor, he added them and, squatting, fanned the flames to get a little warmth. He began to eat some of his food and ponder what had occurred.

It dawned on him that several other crofts had also been in darkness as he'd made his way along the road. Obviously there was mischief afoot but there was no sense in searching for news before daylight. He unhitched Pepper and gave her some grass to nibble, and brought her into the house away from prying eyes. He settled himself beside the warmth of the newly kindled fire, and gradually drifted to sleep.

When he awoke, Angus was surprised to find that it was already morning. He had obviously slept very well. The rain had stopped and Pepper stood patiently beside him, waiting for their day to start.

With some of his hoarded food inside him and a couple of whisky horns in his sporran, Angus saddled Pepper and went to take a look for folk along the road. Nearby and still unharmed was the home of Charlie MacGonigle. They'd not been close friends, but had grown up together, so he drew up at their back door.

Angus didn't want to draw unnecessary attention so he called out gently to the family. It was a while before Charlie himself cautiously came out the back door to see who was there. Seeing it was Angus, he ushered him into the croft.

'Angus, we have to be very careful since the Highland army left the area. They're on the march towards England. A band of thugs are rampaging the area.'

'Do you know who they are?' asked Angus.

'No, they're not local but the word is that the MacCannie boys are the leaders.'

'Yes, I know of them. They're bad news.'

'We have little enough around here without threats from them, demanding we pay them goods or money, or they will torch our houses and drive off our cattle.'

'Bastards!' said Angus.

'They make no distinction between Jacobite and Hanoverian. Pay us or suffer.'

As Angus settled himself by the fire, Charlie continued. 'At first everyone ignored the threat, thinking it was just bluff but four of the thugs returned and your home was not the only one to be gutted and the milk cow driven off.'

'Bad cess to the lot of them!' snorted Angus.

'They could have picked any of us. It was just by chance that they chose your home. We didn't see it happen, and by the time anyone went there, a terrible mess was all we found and no sign of your brother or sisters. We still don't know what happened to them.'

'They must have got away before the thugs arrived. I'll find them,' said Angus, 'and I'll be ready to welcome the thugs if they come back this way.'

Charlie knew Angus was a formidable man and if anybody could take on the marauders it would be him. His family wanted to hear any news Angus carried. They all gathered around Angus and as he shared out his whisky he spoke of Fort William and the news from there. They spoke of Strathnairn and told further stories of the trouble the thugs were causing.

As Angus prepared to leave, Charlie asked him, 'Where do you think your family might have gone?'

'I don't know where they are, but I trust they are safe,' said Angus. 'It was lucky none of the robbers would ever guess where to dig for anything valuable we might have. I've checked the ash trees and it's all undisturbed.' Angus was setting a trap to flush out any informers who might be amongst them. There were no valuables buried anywhere at his house.

'They're a vicious bunch, the MacCannies,' said Charlie, ignoring his comment. 'Their father was a big cattle thief until he was killed five years ago. It was known all over the Highlands that he sold stolen herds somewhere in the north of England.'

Angus nodded. 'I was there a few years ago when he was killed by my nephew Ian Og during a raid. Good riddance to him. His boys were bad ones even then, and it'll be a hard task to rid ourselves of them.'

'Oh, that'll take more than a miracle,' said Charlie, as he followed Angus out to the road.

'The least we can do is try,' said Angus, shaking his head. 'I'd really like to have a go at them. They're a disgrace to decent drovers and Highlanders.' Purposefully, he drew in his breath and said, 'I'll go visit a few more of the local folk and see what they think. I'll let you know.'

'Good luck with that,' said Charlie, as they shook hands. 'Of course, I'll be glad to join you, if it's possible. They did the Tanner's house too, and I think they found money as well. The girls there had to make themselves scarce for days, or they would have been at risk of assault.'

Angus sighed and turned away, but aware of Charlie's eyes on him as he went up the road to the next house.

The MacPhersons were a quiet couple. Two sons had gone south with the Jacobites and their two daughters kept house. Of course they knew his family and Angus was welcomed and questioned for any news he might have of the war.

While they settled before the fire, Angus brought out a whisky horn, and as they sipped the couple told him all they knew about the raids and the MacCannies. The boys had been bullies around Inverness and Strathnairn for years. If they'd known of any buried wealth at Angus's home, it would be gone by this time.

With another sip of his whisky, Angus said, 'Well, it is lucky nobody checked under the stall of the milk cow after she was run off. That could have caused problems, and not just for my family. We would have been left destitute, and the fortunes of Bonnie Prince Charlie and the Jacobite cause would have been at risk.'

As he spoke, he gave them a swift appraising glance and took another sip of his whisky, hoping they would forgive him if they realised his subterfuge and were not guilty.

By the time he returned home, Angus had shared his whisky with several families, and learned much more about the MacCannie thugs. The horns were empty but his plan to deal with the raiders and anyone in league with them was taking shape.

When night fell, he again brought Pepper into the safety of the house. Angus then took a spade and did a bit of digging in several sheltered areas of the ground behind the wee house. This was to strengthen his claims that he had checked the buried treasure. Completing his task, he went inside and settled himself down to sleep by the fire. Gazing into the gently flickering flames, Angus asked the spirits dwelling there to give him some kind of guidance about the family.

He drew his plaid around him and added more wood to the fire. Cheery flames rose up and he took a closer look around him. Despite the raiders' litter, the heart of the room remained. There were several charcoal drawings on the wall. The family had always used charcoal to make pictures. He'd not been very good at it. His strengths were in more practical pursuits, but the girls seemed to be gifted with their drawing. Jean was the best. There was always life in the animals she drew, and he smiled momentarily as he recalled happier times.

The glow from the fire was comforting and he allowed himself to drift into sleep, but it was short-lived. With a start, he awoke. In the light of the dying embers, he stared straight at Jean's wall drawings. Although there was mucky peat ash thrown across them, the message was clear: three cats together, looking out at him, with a glove beside them. His siblings were safe with their cousins, commonly known as the 'Cat Clan', the Mackintoshes at Moy Hall, whose Clan emblem was embossed with their motto *'Touch Not the Cat Bot a Glove'*. With a sigh of relief, he thanked his sisters for their clue. He lay down again and allowed a peaceful and deep sleep to overwhelm him.

When he woke, well refreshed, Angus made great efforts to clean the house and mend any broken furniture. He washed most of the peat ash off the walls, leaving the charcoal clues that his sisters had made. He would stay and buy grain for Anghie while he awaited the return of the MacCannies. His plan was to make sure they did return by spreading false information that would lure them out.

When local folk saw he was back in the family home, several of his neighbours came to call on him. The women generally offered help to clean the place, but in truth both men and women came to hear about the progress of the Jacobite army and Bonnie Prince Charlie. Angus had little current news to offer, but he poured a welcome dram for everyone and said how fortunate it was that he had come home at this time to get grain for the still in Glen Rowan. From time to time, he was asked if the raiders had taken anything valuable. He always said he didn't think so and that nobody had dug up the field, but that they had taken his sister's fiddle that used to hang on the wall.

He also told them he was going to stay for a while to get the place sorted, learn what had happened to the family and prevent anyone from doing any more damage.

As November arrived, the days grew shorter and colder. Angus had the roof mended, and peat and logs gathered in as the first flakes of snow began to dust Strathnairn. Visits to and from the neighbours continued, and he noted those who seemed particularly interested in his own links to the prince.

It was when one neighbour in particular, Hector Robertson, whose two sons were away – but not with the Jacobites – began to take an 'offhand' interest in his digging in the field that Angus felt it was time to put his plan into action. He hoped to save Strathnairn and its people from any further interference from the MacCannie boys. During one of Robertson's visits, he let slip that he was anxious about a casket of gold he was holding for the Jacobites. However, he had at last received a message to get it down to Stirling in the next few days.

When Hector was finally on his way home, Angus went to visit several of his neighbours, those he'd known since he was a youngster and who he knew could be trusted. He told them that the MacCannie boys were likely to turn up in the next couple of days, intent on robbing his house and his field of a great treasure. Working together and with careful planning, they could end their evil reign of terror.

Only three days later, as an icy rain poured down from the grey sky above, Strathnairn was invaded by a lively group of riders. The MacCannie boys had returned and began to shoot their way along the deserted road. Their intention was to strike fear into anyone they encountered. They expected no resistance and met none. Little did they realise they had been watched ever since leaving Inverness. Locals hidden in Angus's field held their fire until the murderous brothers, now wielding spades, gathered together in behind Angus's croft.

The MacCannie boys were so intent on their search of the field that they didn't realise until too late that they were surrounded by angry locals led by Angus. It was short and bloody work, and none of the MacCannie raiders survived. They were all dead before nightfall and were quietly buried together with the use of their own spades in the field where they fell.

Angus welcomed everyone into his house and served generous portions of whisky.

'The MacCannies will do no more harm around here,' said a triumphant Angus. 'And let that be a lesson to any other thugs who may contemplate coming our way. I want to thank you all for your help and the courage you showed.'

There was a loud cheer as everyone raised their mugs and drank to that. Charlie, who was Angus's closest neighbour and had played a major role in the fight, then spoke as he raised his mug again. 'Those MacCannie boys will now do more good in death than they ever did in life, as compost out in that field.'

Another cheer erupted and then some serious drinking and happy banter took over as they celebrated their victory well into the night.

The following day, there was no sign of Hector Robertson or his family at his house in Strathnairn. Feeling in much better spirits, Angus secured the family's house, and set off on a well-rested Pepper for Moy Hall and, he hoped, for his family.

CHAPTER 13

IT WAS A COLD, DANK DECEMBEr day and a very tired
Sarah shivered as she lay beside her younger siblings,
quietly dozing together in bed under a mound of
clothing and hides. She had been trying to sleep, but
her heart was heavy. There were no other women left
in the Glen and she had now become the 'Mammy 'of
her family, both children and adults. Despite her best
efforts to conserve food, the last of the grain was gone,
shared out in a thin gruel. There wasn't anything left
for the whisky-making, and they'd also eaten the last of
the venison strips two days earlier.

Sarah wasn't feeling hungry herself, but her stomach
was upset so she rose, trying not to disturb the others.
In bed they were at least warm. Jimmy and the twins
were almost yellow in their hunger. All were noticeably
thin, their skin clinging to their bones. Sarah had been
noticing these last few weeks that she always felt unwell
in the mornings. Foreboding thoughts were creeping
into her mind, and the possibility of another mouth to
feed was daunting.

She gathered her clothes around her and considered yet again what choices she had to obtain food. Wildlife on the snow-covered hills was scarce. The deer trapped by the fire had been a lucky prize, but few birds and no hares meant the store was now empty, and with a tear in her eye she had to consider that the declining packhorse Sneeshan might be the next casualty of their hunger.

There was only one choice. She must go to the clan's elite, a rich family at Keppoch Castle, and beg for assistance. Times were hard and most of the men would be off with the prince, but they would surely not let a clan family starve. She hadn't been there for a year or two. Keeping an eye on everyone since Mamma died meant she rarely left the glen. The packhorse could carry her up to the castle and would get some feed as well.

Under the pale frost there was little forage for her in the glen. As Sneeshan wearily plodded along the path, Sarah found her mouth watering at the thought of the decent feed she would receive as soon as they reached their destination. There had been rumours that, with most of the family away, the Keppoch cousins were also having a difficult time. People were reluctant to bother them, but Sarah had nowhere else to go.

Within an hour, the beast was ambling through the back gate of the castle. Glad to stop at one of the sheds, Sarah tied Sneeshan beside some feed and thanked the pony. She went to look for Mrs Cameron, and found her in the big warm kitchen.

Seeing her, the housekeeper ladled broth into a bowl and put it on the table with some bread.

'Get that down you,' she said, beckoning her towards

a chair to sit down and eat. 'Have you come for food?'

'Yes, Mrs Cameron. Things are very bad and I'm worried about the young ones. Wee Eileen especially is beginning to fade. There's nothing growing and no animals to be seen.' Tears welled up as Sarah spoke and she stifled a sob.

The older woman put a comforting arm around her. 'Sit for a moment, Sarah. I'll get you a dram.'

'Oh ... I'm not sure I should just now. I've not eaten for some time.'

Mrs Cameron ignored the remark and brought a large cup filled with whisky, and a bannock. She set them on the table beside the soup.

'It must be bad in the glen.'

'Yes, indeed,' Sarah nodded. 'But I hope I can get some food here today. It has been much worse with the men away ... and no news.' She began to cry.

Mrs Cameron patted her shoulder gently. 'Indeed, and I am sure you will leave here with food, but it may cost you something and I think you will be better prepared with the whisky.'

Sarah heard the words, but didn't understand their meaning. She began to take some of the soup before her and picked at the bannock. The whisky was close and she took a sip from the cup.

'When you've finished that,' said Mrs Cameron, 'I'll go and fetch Mr Hector. He's in charge of the house while the family are away.'

'I don't know him. What's he like?'

'You'll just have to judge for yourself.' The house-keeper was clearly not going to give an opinion. 'You get that whisky down you and I'll go and fetch him.'

Sarah was finishing off her bannock and the whisky when the older woman returned, followed by a tall man with a walking stick. As he entered, Sarah rose and curtsied.

Without any social preamble, Mr Hector spoke. 'Mrs Cameron has told me of your situation. You want food. I do know your family, but it's been a long time since I was up in Glen Rowan. Take this candle and come with me.'

He turned to leave the kitchen and added, 'Wait here, Mrs Cameron.'

As Sarah followed, his tone softened. 'I've always liked your family, Sarah. You have certainly blossomed since your mother died.'

'Thank you,' was all that Sarah could think of to say.

'Oh yes, and now I hear you are a woman betrothed. He's a lucky man indeed.'

It was an awkward conversation for Sarah. She could not remember ever meeting Mr Hector before, but followed as he led the way down to the old store in the cellar.

Once inside, he took the candle, used it to light another, and set one on the table and one on a shelf. Sarah almost gasped at the sight before her. There were wooden shelves with jars and boxes of dried meat and vegetables. Hooks on the wall held herbs. In one corner there were several wooden barrels.

Mr Hector spoke. 'We have very little now. Hardly enough to keep the staff fed, but Mrs Cameron assures me you need to feed the little ones.' As he was talking, he picked up a small empty sack and put it on the table. 'Now, let me see … what you would like to fill it with?'

'What can I take?' Sarah asked in anticipation.

'What would be best for you?' He waved his arm around the room.

Sarah's hungry eyes had already spied the strips

of dried venison. She took a handful and laid them on the table. Mr Hector watched her but said nothing, so she took a few more strips. It gave her courage to go to a barrel where a cup lay on top of the oatmeal. She brought the small sack close to it and took five cups of it, one for each of the family at home. When Mr Hector indicated she could have more, she took a second helping for everyone. Looking around, she saw only two kippers and she took one, but again Mr Hector indicated she could put both into the sack.

Some fresh scones caught her eye. They sat on one of the stone shelves beside Mr Hector. He signalled for her to come and fetch them, and she edged herself around between the table and the wall. When she was close enough to reach them, Mr Hector leant forward as if to give her a helping hand, but instead grabbed her arm and pulled her firmly towards him. 'Come here, my lovely. It's time to pay the piper.'

Startled at this unexpected movement, Sarah pulled back and then forward to push him away, but he held her firmly and pushed her face down on the table. While holding her down with one hand he used his other hand to fumble with her plaid and the *lèine* underneath, exposing her naked bottom. It was as he began to lift his own plaid that his grip loosened slightly and Sarah made a desperate attempt to push herself off the table. Hector tried to keep his balance, but with a mighty effort, she shoved him back and this time the table tipped up and they fell together to the stone floor, landing heavily with a crash. There was an ominous silence.

She scrambled off the motionless body and shrank against the wall, stunned and unable to think. Not wanting to spend a moment longer in the cold cellar, she grasped the candle and stumbled back to the kitchen. She tried to call for help, but her mouth was dry and her words died on her lips.

Mrs Cameron noticed the distressed Sarah as she stumbled back into the kitchen. She immediately started to pour out another cup of whisky. 'Are you all right?' she began. 'Did you get food?'

'I think he's dead,' was all that Sarah could say. 'Come see.'

Mrs Cameron and Sarah hastily made their way down to the cellar. The housekeeper breathed a sigh of relief and took Sarah in her arms. 'Thank God! He was a complete bastard. Did he hurt you?' And when Sarah shook her head, the woman again said, 'A complete bastard, you were lucky.'

She paused. 'Now, let me think … do not go near him, Sarah. Gather up your sack and take those scones and the bannocks, and anything else you need. Don't worry about the mess on the floor, I'll take care of that.'

Back in the warmth of the kitchen, a much shaken Sarah sat at the table and began to sip the whisky again. Dazed and confused, she couldn't make sense of what had just happened.

The older woman was mumbling to herself and seemed to be giving a history of the day's events. 'Let me think … you came in the back gate. Good lass. The pony is in the old shed. Nobody will have seen it. So you can head home that same way too when you've finished the whisky.'

Sarah nodded agreement.

'You've to take the sack too. Otherwise people might realise someone was here.' Sarah's grey face broke into a relieved smile.

Mrs Cameron continued. 'And Sarah, you haven't been here. Understand?'

'Oh yes, Mrs Cameron.'

Sarah was worried. 'Are you sure you won't get into any trouble?'

'I won't go and find him for a while, and then I'll call someone to help. It looks like an accident, Sarah, and that's what I shall tell everyone. But you need to get away before anyone returns for their dinner.'

Sarah drained the last drops in the cup and hugged the older woman. 'Thank you and God's blessing on you, Mrs Cameron.'

'A blessing on you too, Sarah. God has already guided your hand.'

Sarah mounted Sneeshan and soon pony and rider were back on the trail towards Glen Rowan.

Later, when one of the family returned to Keppoch, Mrs Cameron went to the cellar for supplies, and returned in an agitated state to say that Mr Hector seemed to have had an accident.

CHAPTER 14

AFTER MANY DAYS OF FROST and snow, the weather cleared and Sarah went out to gather moss at Angus's pool, to use as stuffing for pillows and bedding. The little stream was in full spate, gurgling and chortling as it gushed between the icy grey boulders, coursing impatiently over rocks, before dropping a foot or two into the brown water below. Although the rowan and other mountain trees had lost their foliage, they softened the mountain wind and provided shelter for the moss, which sparkled like emeralds in the mist at the water's edge.

Intent on her task, Sarah didn't hear the rider and packhorse making their way along the track. When she turned, hands overflowing with the soft sponge of green and brown moss, he was there, tall on an unfamiliar horse and towering above her.

'Alistair! You gave me such a fright,' she said, eagerly casting her harvest into the half-full bucket and scrambling up the bank, wiping her hands on the grass as she went.

'I hear you're to be married.' His face carried no expression as he dismounted and came towards her.

Sarah's bright smile of welcome faded. 'You've seen Dadda then …?' It was a half-question.

'I did,' he said, with crushing smoothness. 'He told me he was the happiest man in the world to see his daughter betrothed to such a fine fellow.' He paused. 'And he is indeed a very fine fellow.'

'Aye … he is that.' Sarah's face was now as bland as his own.

'And he'll make a fine job of caring for you.' As he spoke he moved towards her.

'He will,' she acknowledged, retreating a step or two.

'Especially with the winter snow you were so worried about.'

'I was indeed.' She moved back further.

He could contain himself no longer. He had spent the last while since hearing that Sarah was betrothed cursing his lot and damning all women, especially dark-haired ones with intelligent hazel eyes and strong hands. He grabbed her arm tightly and shook it exasperatedly, pushing her backwards against a big boulder.

'Sarah ... what happened?'

He wanted to thrash the life out of her for the anger she had caused him. The memory of Dadda MacDonell's proud face shining with the sweat of a day's march as he told him the happy news of Sarah's betrothal was like a sword piercing his heart, shattering the treasured dreams he'd hoped would come true. Dadda never learned how close he'd come to being punched at that moment, and now it was only those dark eyebrows, lifting like swallow's wings, which stopped Alistair putting his hands around Sarah's neck and throttling the life from her.

She wrenched her arm away but could retreat no further. 'Ouch ... Alistair! That hurt! You weren't there. Dadda just did it, and it was awful.'

'From what he said, you didn't put up much of a fight. Too keen to have anyone who'd take you? A little girl from the hills.' The smoothness of his voice was becoming thin. It was a cruel thing to say and he meant to wound.

'That's not fair. That's not how it was!'

'According to Dadda, you didn't say anything against it.'

'I couldn't,' she protested, adding weakly, 'It was all sort of assumed.'

'Assumed?' His sneer drawled the word out.

'Yes, assumed,' she said flatly. 'First it was the fire. Then Grannie died and instead of everyone going away, they all stayed.' She looked up at him but he said nothing, just stood there glaring at her through narrowed eyes. 'Hamish was very good to Dadda and the others. He helped assemble the coffin and all sorts of things like that. He was very kind to me,' she finished in a whisper.

'So when Dadda asked you ...' he said, in a voice edged with sarcasm, 'you said, "of course. I'd love to be betrothed. I might need a coffin one day."'

'It didn't happen like that. Dadda didn't ask me. He just announced it to everyone there.' There was a hint of despair in her voice.

'Your father said you were as pleased as he was. It didn't sound as if you were dragged unwillingly into a match.' He spoke sternly.

'Well, in a way I suppose I wasn't,' she said.

'There you are!' His words were bitter. 'You wanted it too.'

'I didn't. But if you weren't coming back ...' She left the rest unsaid.

Looking down at her, he shook his head slowly. 'How could you?'

'It was Dadda.' She couldn't find the words to explain her dilemma. 'You know how he can be. He was so sad with Grannie dying and everything, and he was leaving, and I was all alone.'

'All alone?' The tone was of disbelief. 'What about Anghie and the girls and wee Jimmy?'

'Anghie and the others don't count. You know that. I got no message, and no word from you since the day of the fire on the mountain.' It was her turn to be angry. That day had kindled something within her, which had soared like a skylark on a clear summer's day. Little by little as the days passed, she'd had to rein it in until the magic was almost forgotten. Now she was being scolded as if it were her fault. 'You didn't come. Each day Angus said you were coming back and you didn't.' She sniffed and said again, 'You didn't.'

Under fire from those glistening lashes, the last shreds of his resolve faded away. 'I couldn't, Sarah. You know I couldn't. I had to go with the prince to Perth and then to Edinburgh, and we had to fight at Prestonpans. I couldn't get back.'

'Oh yes. I heard about the battle. Even a little girl from the glens heard about the battle. Hamish came up specially and told us. He told us of Archie MacDonald and James Cameron over at Locheil. He told us that Dadda, Roderick and Ranald were unhurt. He also told us that you were all right. But not a word from you,' she finished accusingly.

'Oh, Sarah,' he sighed. 'I would never have left if it were at all possible.'

'You left! I felt it was love, but how could I know?'

He leaned forward, gently taking her hand. 'I told you ...'

'You didn't!' she insisted, leaving her hand in his. 'You said you'd speak to Dadda but then you rode off. You didn't come back or send word or anything. I couldn't know it meant anything to you. You've known lots of lassies.'

'You knew it wasn't like that,' he said gently, putting his arm round her.

'How could I be sure? Even Angus was expecting you, and you didn't come.' She sniffled.

'But we were off to war! You knew I'd come back if I could.'

'I didn't know,' she protested, as tears began to roll down her cheeks.

'Oh please, Sarah, don't cry.' His hand came up and tenderly wiped the tears away.

'I'm NOT crying,' she said defiantly. 'I'm very pleased. I'm betrothed to a very nice man who'll look after me and the baby, and he comes up here quite often to make sure I am all right.'

'THE BABY ...' Alistair was shocked. 'What baby?'

Sarah had accidently gave voice to her inner thoughts. 'I think I am going to have a baby,' she said and then started to sob again.

Almost in a whisper he asked 'My baby?'

It took a moment or two before she spoke. 'I don't know, Alistair.'

'What do you mean ... you don't know. Whose else could it be?'

'One day while you were away, Hamish called to see how I was. He was so caring and loving and one thing led to another... and I was so lonely for you, that it just happened. I'm sorry'

'You're sorry? You're sorry!'

'I am sorry, but I can't change what happened.'

'So, I could still be the father! You don't know for sure I am not the father.'

'No, I don't know for sure, but Hamish will be a good husband for me and a good father for the baby. He won't be off like a shot, leaving me alone, when the prince calls for warriors again.'

'God save us, Sarah, will you stop doing that? I could clout you when you're like that.' His lips kissed her wet cheek.

'Like what?' Her protest was less urgent now.

'Like that, pretending you don't care who you marry. I want to smack you and shake you.' His arms were now enfolding her.

'Go ahead! That's just the sort of thing your kind would do,' she mumbled.

'My kind?' he said smiling.

'Yes, your sort. You force yourself on a helpless girl, and then you don't come back, and when you see her again, you hit her.'

He laughed. 'Oh, Sarah, I'd never do that. Mind you, I might be tempted to take you over my knee and spank you to make you understand.'

'You wouldn't!' There was a glint behind those bright eyes as she looked up at him.

'I might have to.' He nodded with a half-smile, drawing her closer.

'Don't you dare. I'll tell Hamish and he'll have to fight you.'

'He'd lose.' Alistair's voice was now soft and beguiling.

'He wouldn't,' Sarah's reply was almost a whisper.

'He would ... you know he would. Will he fight me if I kiss you?'

'Yes.'

'Will you tell him?' The words were murmured as he kissed her ear.

'Yes,' she lied, as her scalp began to prickle.

'And tell him about this?' His lips caressed her neck, as the breath in her lungs was expelled with the sudden force of a tingling explosion which burst down her spine. 'Oh yes!' she exclaimed in a whisper and turned her lips to his. Once again, lightning coursed through her whole being, mind and body fused with desire and all thought of the frost and snow gone.

Soon they were lying spent, side by side, on the sparkling moss bed, breathing heavily.

'Oh Alistair, I'm freezing. We can't do this.' The enormity of the situation was beginning to seep into Sarah's thoughts.

Alistair brought his head up. 'You can't say this is nothing,' he murmured, kissing her on her mouth again.

She responded enthusiastically but, as his hands again began to fondle her breasts and gently rub her belly, her conscience awoke. 'No Alistair ... We can't, we mustn't.'

'Yes, we can.'

As he gently lowered his lips to her hard pink nipple, Sarah felt the breath leave her lungs. 'It's not fair,' she gasped.

'It's not fair on whom?' He asked as he turned his attention to the other nipple.

'On Hamish ... It's wrong, Alistair.'

'A pox on Hamish,' said Alistair as he watched her adjusting her clothing. 'Can't you forget him for just a few moments?'

'I can't. Dadda has made the arrangement and I can't go against his wishes ... unless ... unless he changes things.' She rose and fetched the overturned bucket and began to refill it with the scattered moss.

As Alistair got up he said. 'We'll explain it to Dadda.'

'Oh, you can't tell him.'

'Why can I not tell him?'

'I would be disgraced.'

'No, you won't. We'll just tell him that it was a mistake and that you were too afraid to say anything.'

She shook her head sorrowfully. 'He wouldn't believe that.'

'Why not? Who would be afraid of Dadda?'

'You're right. He's the gentlest man alive, except for maybe Ranald. You should have seen them when Grannie died. They were so sad. The betrothal made them live again.'

'And Hamish,' Alistair coiled a black curl of Sarah's hair around his finger, then crushed it several times, watching as it sprang back into shape. 'Does he know you only took him because Dadda put you in an awkward position?'

'He just loves me and the hard part is that I love him too. Not like us, but like family. He is such a good man.'

'Not like me?'

'I don't know what you are. Sometimes I think you're not good, though you've always been good to me, especially when Mamma died.'

'Yes. I think that was when I realised that I properly loved you, and only you. You were such a little thing, and there you were with the whole family on your shoulders.' As if to express his point further, he put his arm around her, but nimbly she went and gathered up her bucket of moss.

'Well, they all helped and Grannie Morag still had her senses then, so it wasn't too bad.' She paused, then asked him, 'What will we do?'

He adjusted his saddle pack to make room for her behind him. 'I'll just have to straighten things out with your Dadda. I'll talk to him when I get back and it'll be fine.'

'What about Hamish?' Sarah asked.

'What about Hamish?' It was Hamish himself who spoke.

The gushing of the little waterfall had masked the sound of approaching riders. Hamish and Ian Og were together on Sneeshan.

Fortunately, Sarah was hidden behind the big boulder, so the newcomers didn't see the blush which swept up from her neck, and by the time she appeared with the moss bucket, no trace of her discomfort was apparent.

'I was just saying what a lucky man you are.' Alistair turned to face the newcomers with a warm smile of greeting. Ian Og was already on the ground and the pair hugged warmly.

With a cheerful grin, Hamish went over and kissed Sarah, then nodded to Alistair. 'Maybe I should be concerned that you're here alone with my fiancée.'

'Oh, indeed you should,' agreed Alistair. 'I was heading for the croft when I spied her, so I delayed a wee bit. What time were you expecting me?'

'The message only said sometime today, and we knew you'd not be sorry to take a rest if we were late. We were up at the still and got some of the whisky organised for Angus.'

'Good. We'll need some of that for cover.'

'So what's the plan, Alistair?' Ian Og sounded keen.

'We are going to rob a courier.'

CHAPTER 15

AFTER SETTING OUT ON A clear freezing morning at sunrise, Torquil MacLeod had already rounded the end of the great Loch Ness by noon, and crossed the river that wound its way down to Inverness and the North Sea. General Wade's fine new road was not far behind him. It had been a tiring journey across snow-covered country from the west, but he was within a half day of his destination: Culloden House, the home of Duncan Forbes, the Lord President of the Scottish Council.

For most of the journey he had taken care to avoid settlements, meeting few people along the way. In the past hour there had been several other travellers making their way towards Inverness, but he'd kept his distance and only one distant rider had followed him off the main road. This solitary horseman was beginning to cause him concern. There had been no obvious attempt to narrow the mile or so between them, but MacLeod could feel his presence, like a cold wind blowing on the back of his neck. He didn't sit easy in his saddle until eventually the brown phantom of man and horse turned off on a side track, heading in a different direction.

Getting closer to his destination, MacLeod remained alert. When he heard raucous shouts ahead, he quickly reined in his horse to a stop and drew his pistol.

Two highlanders came running along the side of a small river, plaids flapping untidily in the wind. One man was lanky and red haired, the other compact and dark. They held their arms stiffly behind them. Gradually he could make out their words. Each blamed the other. So intent were they on arguing back and forth, they seemed to be quite unaware of his presence, but the man from Skye was a cautious traveller at the best of times, so, to be on the safe side, he waited.

As the pair approached, it became apparent that their hands were bound behind them and they were roped together. The smaller of the two wanted to stop and untie the rope. The other was saying there was no time and kept pulling him forward.

Before MacLeod could consider the likely danger to himself from these two, a red-coated rider came into view, leading two packhorses and spurring his own to catch up with the runaways. His booming voice easily bridged the gap between them. '*Stop them!*' He yelled in English. '*Don't let them get away!*'

For the first time, the highlanders noticed the traveller ahead of them and instead of turning to avoid him, they threw themselves forward, calling out 'He will kill us, sir! Don't let him take us. He's a devil, sir!' The younger and darker of the two highlanders ignored the pistol pointing at him and looked up beseechingly at the soberly attired stranger.

'He's going to take us to see the Lord President himself. Sir, he's a mad man.'

'Stand back,' MacLeod spoke sharply to them in Gaelic and, without lowering his guard, took a careful look at the man riding towards them.

The newcomer was dressed as a subaltern in Sir John Guise's Regiment of Foot which was first founded in 1688. Regiments were named after the colonel who founded them, until 1751 when a royal warrant was issued which provided that in future regiments would no longer be known by the name of the founding colonel. This subaltern was not wearing his formal wig, and his unpowdered hair was tied back under a tricorn hat.

When he was close enough, MacLeod called to him. *'They seem a pretty pair, sir. How did you lose them?'*

Alistair made a perfunctory bow from his saddle and continued to speak in the loud English manner he had affected. *'I thankee, sir, for your assistance. When my horse stumbled, the rope dislodged and they ran away. I was most vexed.'* He looked down at the two men. *'They may be a sorry-looking pair, but I'll say one thing for them: they can move very quickly when they've a mind.'*

'Don't let him take us, sir. We're Lochaber men and he's kidnapped us.'

The Skye man critically surveyed the other rider for a moment. Although he was about his own age and wearing a red uniform, he looked ungainly in the saddle. MacLeod shook his head with a mixture of tolerance and disbelief. *'I fear you are but lately resident in these wild parts, sir, or you would have learned never to underestimate the native highlander. Most have lived in isolation so long that they can always be trusted to surprise one.'*

'He's kidnapped us, sir. And those are our horses.'

'You are very perspicacious, sir,' Alistair acknowledged gruffly. *'I am learning this. I thought I had bound them*

well enough.' As he spoke he climbed down from his horse with stiff legs and took charge of the long ropes to which Hamish and Ian Og were attached. He apparently bound them more closely at the wrist and waist, before attaching the loose ends firmly to his saddle and remounting.

MacLeod had not re-holstered his pistol. *'Before we proceed, sir, may I enquire what right you have to detain these men? They say they are from Lochaber and that you have kidnapped them.'*

'They may well say that.' The loud voice echoed between the trees. *'I'm not at all surprised. I have indeed kidnapped them, but only in the name of the King.'*

'Did you capture them on your own?'

'Yes, I did and I am bringing them to Mr Forbes. He will know what's to be done with them.'

The crass stupidity of such a journey was not lost on MacLeod, and before he could restrain his curiosity, he replied, *'I am amazed at your enterprise, sir. Taking two prisoners on such a journey is quite a task.'*

'It is quite a task and since I captured them I have been forced to stay alert and it was in a moment of inattention that they escaped.'

'But still, have you the right to take them?' Torquil MacLeod was a stickler for the law. It was one of his disagreements with the rebellion, which he considered unlawful.

'Oh yes.' Alistair nodded to emphasise the point. *'The authorities in Lochaber have been trying to catch these two for months now, and at last they found the evidence.'*

'They have evidence?' It was a question.

'Whisky.'

'Whisky?' MacLeod couldn't keep the astonishment out of his voice. *'You hold the King's commission, sir. You*

are not a bailiff to be taking whisky smugglers and stillers to the Lord President of the Council.'

With a look of shocked horror on his face, Alistair immediately reined in his horse and his hand fumbled towards his pistol. *'Sir, you must be a wizard in league with the devil to know that.'*

His new companion quickly shook his head with a smile and raised a hand, palm outwards towards the firearm pointed at him. *'You need not fear that I am the devil, sir. Your prisoners have loose tongues.'*

Alistair's look of appalled astonishment faded into a wry smile of realisation, and he slowly nodded his acceptance of the truth of the stranger's words.

'Yes, indeed. I have a great deal to learn. I am going to see the Lord President, although I was hoping the visit would not become common knowledge. There are plenty of rogues who would be happy to prevent these two reaching his house at Culloden and here am I, forced to trust a perfect stranger. Although, sir, you have an honest face.'

Flattered despite himself, MacLeod shook his head in disbelief and raised his eyes to heaven. *'Ah sir, despite your uniform, you are still naive. In these parts, you should not take an honest face as any recommendation at this time. The rebellion is turning the head of many a good man.'* Seeing the look of concern on Alistair's open, trusting face, he added, *'Be easy. You are indeed safe with me, and it is my own intention to travel in that direction. But before I agree to assist you in your task, I hope you will tell me why you must trouble Mr Forbes?'*

Despite his misgivings, Torquil MacLeod was considering the advantages of having company for the final few miles of the journey. The little package of letters prickling against the skin on his back was a prize that should not be allowed to fall into rebel hands.

They contained secret information about clan movements that had been gathered from spies working for the crown.

Travelling with this pompous red-coated officer would make him a much more difficult pigeon to pluck. On the other hand, keeping an eye on two wily whisky distillers would entail a loss of time, particularly if they were walking.

'It's a slow road to travel with two prisoners on foot,' MacLeod mused.

Alistair nodded in agreement. *'I'd tie them to their own packhorses, but I am getting tired now and couldn't trust them not to destroy the evidence.'*

'A wise move, I'm sure, but perhaps if I were to assist you to keep a watchful eye on your two men, we can, between us, get them to Culloden House all the more quickly.'

'Your offer is very tempting sir. It is a miracle that we have travelled this far, and I daresay we have the uprising to thank for that with the clansmen marching south, but I do not wish to tempt providence further.

Once it was agreed, the two prisoners were allowed to mount their horses. Not an easy task with hands bound behind them, but under MacLeod's watchful pistol, Alistair's cupped hands provided a mounting step and within a few moments each was set upon his pack saddle. There was plenty of rope bound around them, which appeared to restrict all but the slightest movement.

Alistair clicked his tongue to encourage his horse into action, and as the group took the trail towards Culloden House, he told his new companion the story that had been concocted during the hasty ride from Glen Rowan. His 'prisoners' had put the final neat cosmetic touches to his clothing and hair, only a few minutes before their quarry rode into view, signalling it was time for the charade to begin.

'*You see,*' Alistair boomed, '*I didn't travel up to Fort William with Captain Swetenham and the rest of my regiment, so I missed the action at High Bridge and what followed. My colonel at the fort felt that, as I was waiting on my regiment to get there it might be appropriate for me to undertake special duties. So in order to teach me about the countryside, he seconded me to the local excise officers.*'

For a moment Torquil MacLeod allowed an uncharitable thought to cross his mind that the colonel might have been very pleased to be relieved of the company of this loud novice.

'*He also felt that, as I am not fully conversant with these wild areas, I should see them first hand and perhaps be of assistance to the excisemen on my travels. Indeed, it has so proved. These two had been cocking a snook at the authorities in Lochaber for a number of years prior to my arrival. By chance, during manoeuvres, the local exciseman found their whisky still during my visit, and said he would bring it to the attention of the chieftain, but I felt it my duty to point out that this chieftain was the head of the notorious Cameron clan.*'

'*It was the senior local excise officer in consultation with the colonel who suggested that the only recourse was for me to bring the matter to the attention of the Lord President directly. Then I captured these two on the way. Now he may not only bring these two to book, but also the chief, Locheil himself.*'

MacLeod listened attentively as Alistair continued.

'*Of course, the local man would have been only too glad to undertake the mission, but he rightly assured me, and the colonel agreed, that he would be too junior to undertake such a matter, and that I would be the appropriate person for such a task.*'

'*I can well understand this.*' MacLeod nodded his agreement. '*But I fear that my lord Forbes will have many other and more pressing charges to bring against the head of the Cameron clan. He may not be too anxious to deal with two whisky makers.*'

Alistair continued, '*He has been very active in the pursuit of local revenues and excise these many years, and despite the current unrest he may wish to have information for when this matter is settled. I have taken every detail in my notebook and it is this in particular I am anxious to present to him.*' He brought out a slim leather-bound notebook from within his cape and held it up triumphantly.

'*I'm sure Mr Forbes will be most grateful for any observations you may have on this matter.*' MacLeod was beginning to rue his decision to travel with this tenderfoot, but reminded himself that it was only for a mile or two further and it provided the best protection for his own mission.

In great detail, Alistair told how he'd spent a number of weeks walking, riding and sailing between many of the Hebridean islands. He had spoken to chieftains and tacksmen, ministers and elders, and the list within his notebook contained confidential information from people who would be sorely embarrassed to declare publicly at this time their support for King George. Some were waiting to see if the French would fulfil their promises to the young Charles Edward Stuart. Others felt the conflict was among strangers and they wanted nothing to do with either side, but feared tax or retribution, whichever side won.

As he listened, MacLeod knew that such information was bound to be more useful at this time of uncertainty than two admittedly cheerful whisky distillers, who, like pilgrims of old, were telling stories to each other in order to pass the time while they travelled towards Culloden.

After a while one of the prisoners began telling the story of the water horse, or kelpie as it was better known. It lived in the great grey waters of Loch Ness, and fell in love with a fair maiden who tilled a field by the shore, not far from the track they had walked along that very day.

Despite his grand clothing and fine education, Torquil MacLeod was a son of the Highlands and the magic of the story began to transport him into that other time where kelpie princes took on human form and wooed beautiful women.

'What's he talking about? My Gaelic is very poor, I'm afraid,' Alistair's words cut into the vision of the raven-haired beauty in Torquil MacLeod's mind, and it took a moment before he understood what was being said.

'He's always prattling about something, but I only catch a word here and there. That's another reason the commander wished me to work with the excisemen. He said I would be of assistance if I could understand more of the correspondence he deals with. But it's an ugly language with its "hochs" and "hoos" and "haggises".'

By this time MacLeod was finding it difficult to view the foolish smile of his new companion with much charity. The magic picture of the story was now like a dream disturbed, the broken shards of a mirror allowing only a fragmented picture, and the weather was turning colder and threatening more snow. To prevent himself becoming very short with Alistair, he asked him more about his work in the Highlands, and began to receive a detailed account of the layout of houses and estates from Achnacarry to Ardtornish and Glencoe to Skye.

It began to dawn on MacLeod what a prize such a notebook would indeed be for the Lord President, who had been working these past months to try and contain the uprising.

Astonished, he asked. *'Did you visit all these places?'*

'Oh not all, but I did ask the excisemen and others about each place and wrote it in as much detail as I could. One can never be sure when such information will be useful. It means I have full details about these two and their still and the routes they generally take over the hills.' Alistair was the picture of self-satisfaction. *'One has to be very thorough if one wishes to see the matter safely through the courts. It must be written down in minute detail as close as possible to the time of the events to retain the accuracy in one's account. I found that most people would disregard me because my Gaelic is poor, but I made sure that each fact was as accurate as possible.'*

'So you have knowledge of the smuggling tracks over the mountains?'

'Not all, by any means, but the ones across Breadalbane and Rannoch, where they can drive an army of laden ponies.'

'Perhaps the Lord President will be very interested in your notebook, maybe even more so than these two loons. I am impressed by your diligence.'

'Yes,' Alistair acknowledged. *'The commander says I am constantly amazing him.'*

Ian Og was still talking away to Hamish and began to tell him another story. With his hands tied behind him, it was difficult to give his usual dramatic flourishes, but his voice conveyed the cold and misery of that night sixty years ago, when the heaviest snow in years lay up to eight feet high on the mountain tracks.

MacLeod was just picturing the snow falling unabated when suddenly, both Ian Og and Hamish kicked their horses into action. The startled animals leapt forward. The rope holding the pair to their captor broke free. The two were making good their escape before MacLeod could draw his pistol. When he was able to level the length of his barrel towards them, he found Alistair hovering like a demented fly in the line of fire, shouting at the pair to come back, before persuading his horse to follow the two fugitives, and calling back to MacLeod, *'They won't get far.'*

With anger in his heart, MacLeod felt honour bound to follow him. It was a consequence of his own persuasion that the two scoundrels had been allowed to ride on their horses, although he felt aggrieved that their security had obviously relied on a poorly knotted rope. Coming around the edge of the gully he was just in time to see Alistair wildly brandishing his sword and following the trail into a copse of bushes, shouting dire threats as he disappeared.

Holding his pistol at the ready, MacLeod followed cautiously. The sounds ahead were muffled, but he could still hear Alistair's shouts, when suddenly a plaid was flung over his head, pulled tightly to pinion his arms and he was yanked off his horse with a thud. On the ground, winded, he felt his pistol wrenched from his grip and heard the Gaelic storyteller gently apologising, 'You look like a decent man, sir, but we cannot let you take us to Mr Forbes.'

While he was getting his breath back, he could hear thuds and expletives a few yards away, before Alistair stopped shouting and there was silence.

The two fugitives began to discuss their next move. It sounded as if the red-coated subaltern had received poor fare and was unconscious. The storyteller was for tying up the two of them and making good their escape with the whisky. The other wanted to check for valuables.

There was the sound of rustling and fumbling which Torquil took to be a search of the redcoat. He would have been astonished if he could see the two fugitives muddying up the hair of a grinning Alistair, while he was stripping off his borrowed finery and turning out the pockets. A hapless blackbird had been sacrificed to provide blood for the edge of the victim's scalp and a smear around his nose. Except for the broad smile, he looked as if he'd been in a brawl and had given a good account of himself.

Within the darkness of the rancid-smelling plaid, MacLeod cursed his luck for falling in with them. He had a couple of Scottish merks in his pouch which might not be considered very much in the pocket of a prosperous Edinburgh merchant, but these coins were not base metal and could last a frugal Highland family many months. He felt his shoes being removed and inspected. He suspected these men had never worn shoes. At best, rough cuarans would meet their needs. He heard the storyteller say, 'These could fetch a tidy sum in Inverness, and the breeks. There wouldn't be much for a red coat, but these look fine. The shirts though would sell well also.'

There was some groaning from the redcoat as if they were stripping him down and searching him. 'A shilling and two groats!' Ian Og exclaimed with a delighted squeak.

'Don't forget that notebook,' Hamish said gruffly, acting his part to the full. 'That could hang us all.'

Then it was Torquil's turn. He tried to defend himself, but the two men were more than a match for him, removing his breeches and hose without any difficulty. He hoped this would be enough for them. But his heart sank when he heard the storyteller say, 'I fancy that shirt. My Mary would like it.'

They tied his legs carefully before removing the plaid from around his upper body. As each took an arm and undressed him, he sighed. There was no chance of escape. He could see that the senseless subaltern too was undressed, but his breeches and topcoat lay discarded on the ground.

With an appreciative 'mmhmm' the storyteller ran his fingers over the shirt and pulled it on. 'Aye, Mary will like this, all right.'

It was the other tall, gruff red-haired highlander who grasped the pouch of letters beside his skin and shook them under MacLeod's nose. 'Aha! What have we here?'

'What do you think?' He triumphantly showed them to Ian Og. 'There'll be money in these.'

At this point Alistair began to groan loudly and cursed intemperately about what he would do to the scoundrels when he caught up with them. There would be no place to hide in the whole of Lochaber, and they would be hanged outside the fort as a warning to others. Then he was quiet again.

'He's not very happy.'

'No, the pompous fool.'

The comments of the two were echoed in Torquil MacLeod's heart, as he worried about his precious cargo of letters. He held his breath. Surely these vagabonds could not read English?

Ian Og held one upside down and looked carefully at the writing. 'What do you think they say?' Hamish asked.

'I don't know.'

'Maybe there's money in it, paper money,' Hamish suggested.

'You can't have paper money. What good would it be?'

'I don't know, but I know you have special paper with writing on it that is like money. It's a promise. I've seen it before,' said Hamish.

MacLeod groaned as he watched the storyteller tear open the seal and show it to the other. 'Do you think there is money in here? Looks like ordinary writing to me.'

Hamish brought it to MacLeod. 'Is this money?'

Wearily, MacLeod shook his head. 'No, of course not, it's just letters.'

'Letters?'

'Yes, just letters. There's a girl getting married at Culloden and her relatives are all sending her letters congratulating her.'

'But why did you keep it secret?' queried Ian Og.

'I didn't keep it secret. I just didn't want to lose them in case I was robbed.'

If Ian Og noticed the irony, he ignored it. 'There might be money in some of them?'

'No.'

'Look ... this one. Is this one money?'

Hamish passed another letter to Ian Og who scanned it carefully before handing it on. They squinted at and examined each letter before getting the bound man to assure them that there was no paper money of any kind in it, and then discarding it.

Alistair's grumbles grew quiet.

When all the letters had been scrutinised and questions asked, Hamish said, 'I'm getting tired of this. If we don't go now, we'll get caught. Someone's bound to find us. Leave these two.'

'They might be here for hours,' said Ian Og, climbing up on Torquil's horse and gathering the rope for one of the pack animals.

Hamish mounted Alistair's horse and took the rope of the second packhorse. 'Won't do them any harm.' He kicked the horse forward.

'Wait, wait. What about my plaid?' Ian Og asked.

'Leave it. You've got the shirt. It'll buy you three plaids.'

As he passed Alistair's crumpled form, Hamish gave him a kick with his bare foot. 'And as for you, I've a mind to run you through with your own sword.' He raised the blade, but Ian Og prodded his horse into action saying, 'C'mon. There's no time for that. We've got a long way to go before we get to Stirling.'

The Skye man waited until the men and beasts were gone, and he felt safe to move. It was a time for both cheer and misery. He was still in one piece and the precious letters were safe, if somewhat dishevelled like himself. The loss of his purse was an inconvenience, not a major blow. Even the loss of the horse would delay him only a short time. But without his clothes, he felt a sorry spectacle, and he must now walk naked in the snow the rest of the way to the Culloden estate. It would hardly take more than an hour, but it was likely to be one of the longest journeys he had taken in his life. He sighed and gathered up the letters, which were scattered around the clearing.

Groans began again to emanate from Alistair's inert form. They were mixed with colourful expressions of what he would do to all whisky distillers and their unfortunate offspring. As he held his head with one hand and patted his body with the other, he promised a lurid fate for the thieves who had stolen his precious notebook.

The tirade suddenly stopped as Alistair stared at MacLeod. *'They took everything of yours. It was a bad day for you when you fell in with us.'*

Slowly he rose to his feet and looked at the hapless Skye man. *'We'll both have to shift on our bare feet, but here, take my coat and the breeches. I'll take that plaid. It'll serve me right for my inattention and the trouble I have caused you.'*

The burning anger which Torquil was nurturing in his heart against this foolish lieutenant melted. His rueful concern and the immediate offer of his clothing was proof against any outburst. Despite his idiocy, the man had a warm spirit.

'Aye, go on then. I'll take your clothes. And we had better get going or we'll freeze to death.'

CHAPTER 16

A STEADY ICY RAIN WAS falling by the time the two barefoot travellers were within sight of Culloden House. There was little conversation between them. Despite the generous gift of the red uniform, Torquil MacLeod was silently berating himself for having fallen in with such a nincompoop. From time to time, Alistair speculated aloud what his commander, Scott, would do to him when he learned of the incident. At these moments, his unwilling companion clamped his lips together in order to prevent his own thoughts escaping in words.

Several uniformed men armed with muskets guarded the entrance gates to the Culloden estate, and the two were cautiously assessed as they entered. On hearing that Mr MacLeod and his companion, Lieutenant Corbet, were here to visit Lord President Forbes, two guards escorted them towards the house. This was the time for Alistair to make his excuses. His luck had held well with a stranger, but Forbes and others in his household would likely recognise him as a nephew of Keppoch. Once again feigning the idiot Englishman, he said, '*I fear the Lord President will not wish to meet me in this sorry attire and without my captives. Can you ask one of these fellows to direct me to the staff quarters or any place where I may find something more suitable for such an audience?*'

Raising his eyes to heaven, MacLeod translated this, and one of the men beckoned Alistair to follow him, and they headed to the rear of the house.

Seeing 'Lieutenant Corbet' go, MacLeod breathed a sigh of relief. Despite all the setbacks, he approached the main door of Culloden House with his precious correspondence complete, if not exactly intact.

Forbes himself came to the door to welcome him and greeted him with astonishment. 'What happened to you, Torquil? And look at your clothes!' He turned to his butler. 'John, we need some clothing for Mr MacLeod. But first bring two large drams to the dining room, and ask Mrs Sinclair to bring some food for our friend.'

With much relief, MacLeod followed him and laid the untidy bundle of letters on the table before sitting down. 'They're all there, Duncan, but for a while I doubted whether you would receive any of them.' As he sipped the whisky and ate the food Mrs Sinclair put before him, he unburdened himself of all the trials and tribulations of his journey.

Alistair, in the servant's quarters at the other end of the house, continued to play the ignorant Englishman. Fortunately, no one guessed that this irritatingly loud, grubby man was a spy, and with insincere smiles offered him the meanest of the available clothes. He took a *lèine* and breeks and cuarans for his feet, but threw Ian Og's plaid around his shoulders, saying that it would be his penance until he returned to Fort William and faced the wrath of fearsome Commander Scott.

The hunger in his stomach could not be ignored, even though he could hear the servants planning to make a fool of him. He picked up two potatoes, which he hoped were difficult to sabotage. They were rather hot and he jumped when they burned his fingers. His audience barely concealed their amusement, but he ate them slowly, one by one, and found no unpleasant surprises. They were also a good excuse to give his false loud voice a rest.

After a while, with his elbows on the table, mumbling quietly to himself, he seemed to settle down and, with his chin cupped in his hands and eyes closed, looked to be asleep. The servants began to ignore him and got on with their own chores and gossiped together.

None of them took any notice when he mumbled from time to time. He gathered potatoes and several bannocks from the table and hid them under his grubby plaid. Suddenly, Alistair froze. 'Moy Hall' had been mentioned. There was word that the prince was there. Alistair cleared his throat and continued mumbling, while listening intently. They were expecting a band of soldiers from Inverness the following day who were tasked with capturing the prince. Some of the men present, who knew the Moy Hall estate, were going with them. The rebellion would soon be over.

After a while, an English-speaking servant came carrying the red uniform with the message. '*Mr Forbes knows you must return to Fort William and Commander Scott as soon as possible. To save you the walk into Inverness, he'll let you take a horse which you can leave with Hugh MacInnis beside Fort George and one of the men will collect it tomorrow. You can get another horse there.*'

The shining gratitude which glowed in Alistair's face was not feigned as he sent his reply with the servant. *'I thankee, Lord Forbes, for your gracious assistance. The stories I have heard about your generosity are not unfounded. I shall leave immediately and face whatever rebuke the commander may have for me.'*

Alistair donned again the red-coat uniform, and gathered up the plaid. With loud expressions of gratitude, he picked up some slices of meat and several more bannocks from the kitchen table, then allowed himself to be escorted to the stable. No doubt, in the course of their correspondence, Mr Forbes would learn that Commander Scott had never heard of Lieutenant Corbet, but that was for the future. The job of ensuring that Mr MacLeod had no knowledge of having been robbed was complete. Alistair had read the letters and copied the information in them into his notebook.

Despite his satisfaction with the job done, Alistair did not allow his guard to drop for several miles. Silently he apologised to the horse beneath him for sitting so awkwardly and bouncing so jumpily, but he felt such a riding style might be the difference between success and discovery. At last, he stopped beside a big rock and waited for a few minutes as if taking a rest, before ducking into the scrubby bushes.

It wasn't long before a completely different Alistair emerged, wearing his own clothes and leading his own horse from the hiding place he had agreed with Hamish and Ian Og. Once the food, red uniform and all the clothing donated by Mr Forbes were stored in a linen sack, he made sure there were no suspicious watchers. Leading the borrowed horse, he turned and made haste towards Inverness.

Night was falling when Mr Hugh MacInnis was approached by a ragged local child, leading a horse and carrying a note for Mr Forbes which thanked him for the use of the animal, and saying that Lieutenant Corbet had fortunately met with a party of soldiers who were leaving for Kilcumin immediately and he would be joining them.

At the same time, two horsemen leading two pack animals could be seen halting beside the snowy track, at the fork leading towards Strathnairn. Alistair joined them.

'Thank God you're safe, Alistair. We were worried about you. So, what happens now?' Ian Og asked. 'Are we were heading down Wade's road.'

'Everything's changed,' said Alistair. 'The kitchen staff said the prince is at Moy Hall, and there will be an attack tomorrow to capture him.'

'Tomorrow!' Ian Og was shocked. He turned his horse. 'Let's go then!'

'No, no! It's not as easy as that,' said Alistair. 'The attack may just be the servants' gossip. It felt real, but I couldn't ask questions. We still have jobs to do. I've got to get the information from the letters back to the clan, and we need to make sure everyone is safe and well in the glen.'

'They'll be fine,' Ian Og was eager. 'Sarah always manages. We have to save the prince.'

'Wait, wait,' said Alistair. 'It could be a wild goose chase. Apart from the gossip, there was no other sign of an attack.'

'Yes,' Hamish. 'And I have to get back home. I've been away for nearly a week. My mother will be climbing up the walls. You know what she is like well enough. It has to be tonight or at the latest tomorrow morning.'

'Well, nobody needs me,' Ian Og said. 'I'll go. I can make good time. There's cousins on the estate who'll know me. I've met them a few times.'

'Yes ... That's not a bad idea,' Alistair agreed, and before he could say any more, Ian Og was off riding swiftly down the Strathnairn road.

Alistair watched him go, then turned to Hamish. 'Well, I reckon he'll do it fine.' He urged his horse into a walk. 'We'd better get going too.'

Once they were moving, he asked, 'And how is your mother? You know there's talk of a siege at the fort. What will she do then?'

'Well, she says it's her home now and she isn't going to be turned out just because there's some squabble going on.'

'Oh dear,' Alistair laughed. 'Some squabble, eh? She's a tough old soul!'

'I hope so. She doesn't want to go back in with the Inverness cousins. My sisters are all safely away in service and she wouldn't want to demean herself by coming up to Glen Rowan.' Hamish sighed. 'And ... I think she's taken a fancy to one of the fort soldiers. There's no telling what she'll do next.'

'Oooh,' said Alistair, with an indrawn breath and a shake of his head. 'That could be awkward, couldn't it? What do the Maryburgh neighbours think?'

'I daren't ask. Not sure I want to know. They're decent enough to me, but lots of them have links with the fort. Anyway, I'll ask her this evening when I get there. Maybe in a couple of days, I'll be able to get up to Glen Rowan and see how things are with Sarah.'

'Aye,' nodded Alistair. 'This fight affects everything, and the government sympathisers' attack on Morvan has really pushed things. That's why we need the information from the letters urgently. With yon Campbell of Argyll on their side, it'll have to be a serious assault on the fort, if we're going to get a decent chance of bringing it down.'

Hamish wondered. 'How are they doing at Corran?' 'Supply ships keep getting through. We've been pecking away at it for months. Those wee cannons down at the narrows are just not good enough, and there's a shortage of mortars. We're lucky sometimes. Managed to sink one a couple of weeks ago and there was another big one which sailed onto the far rocks trying to avoid us,' Alistair laughed, then rubbed his chin ruefully. 'Most of them get past easily enough. The devils had the cheek to come ashore a couple of weeks ago, and torch some houses along the loch side.'

'We have to keep trying to stop them.' Hamish was worried.

'Well ...' Alistair paused. 'There's supposed to be some cannon on the way from Stirling. Lots of promises from the French also over the past few months, but nothing has come yet. At least the soldiers have abandoned Fort Augustus, and they did so in a hurry so maybe we can get guns from there. We could give Fort William a hard time. As you say, it won't be easy. But I'd like to try, while we wait for the French.'

'Aye,' Hamish mumbled resignedly. 'If they come at all. In the meantime, that Captain Scott is a hard bastard. Maryburgh and the surroundings will probably take a pasting from the fort. I can't think how my mother will cope.' He sighed. 'Squabble or no squabble, at least if it turns ugly, up in the glen she should be safe.' He paused. 'IF she'll go.'

'Yes,' said Alistair. 'They'll look after her if she goes.

It'll be good to see them tonight,' he added. 'Sarah was looking well last week.'

'Aye. She's a bonnie lass. I'm sorry not to be heading up there with you.'

'I've brought some food from Forbes' kitchen. That should help for a while.' As Alistair spoke he reined his horse to a halt and took a look around. 'I don't think there's anyone following. Best we get a move on. Keppoch needs those names tonight. Hopefully then I can get an idea of what's likely to happen.

'When will I see you then, Alistair?'

'As soon as I get the chance, Hamish, I'll aim for Maryburgh, and let you know if the siege is likely. We'll call it a kestrel, and if you need to get your mother to safety, you'll get a chance to do it.'

'As I said … if she'll agree.' With a sigh, and a final wave to Alistair, Hamish turned his horse towards Fort William.

CHAPTER 17

Two DAYS EARLIER, Angus's spirits were lifting as he approached Moy Hall, the Mackintosh estate where he'd grown up. The usual bustle and clamour of the place was notably missing, though. The few people he could see moved furtively, as though afraid of watchful eyes, and they spoke in whispers. The past weeks were fresh in his mind as he looked around. He knew he had read the messages on the wall correctly when he saw his sister Jean and his brother Roddy leaning over the newly kindled fire, hands spread towards its warmth. His spirits lifted and his worries subsided.

It was only two months since Pepper had borne him down the trail from Glen Rowan heading for the family home at Strathnairn, but it seemed much longer. He remembered how his heart had stopped when he'd found the damaged house. At first there were no obvious clues as to the safety of the family, but his anxiety had been relieved somewhat when he saw Jean's drawing of three cats and a glove. A symbol of the motto of the Mackintosh clan.

His brother Roddy was the first to see him and immediately rushed over to embrace him with tears of joy in his eyes. Jean soon joined the joyous reunion. As they made their way towards the house itself Angus's mind was flooded with memories. It was here he had learned to make all kinds of useful baskets from willow and other shrubs, thus gaining his nickname, 'Angus Sticks'.

He had also learned to make whisky, and often joined the long whisky trains heading south on the old drove roads. Nowadays, whenever he visited Moy Hall, he would meet up with old friends and get grain for his Glen Rowan still. There was rarely difficulty in getting a load and sending it to Anghie, who was now his main assistant.

His first love had been the daughter of the senior estate supervisor, the tacksman. He often talked to her while she was at the spinning wheel but never proclaimed his feelings because, as a penniless estate worker, he could never hope to meet her family's expectations. When his dear sister Mary was betrothed to Duncan Ban from Glen Rowan, he knew it was his chance to go with her and start a new life there. Now, deep within his heart, he knew that Sarah's vision was a message for him and there would be a challenge to be met at Moy Hall.

When he arrived at the Hall, he was greeted by Lady Mackintosh herself. Angus was not a stranger and very welcome anytime but especially now, because most of the menfolk had gone with Lord Mackintosh to serve the Hanoverians while she and the remaining workers opted for the other side, the Jacobite cause. Sitting with the lady in the main room, a cheery fire in the hearth, a welcome dram on the table, he was brought into the secret that the twenty-five-year-old 'Bonnie Prince' was now living at Moy Hall. Everyone on the estate was on the alert for his safety and Angus gave thanks to his sister Mary for Sarah's vision.

It was almost dark when his nephew Ian Og came galloping at full speed into the estate and up to the hall, the bearer of bad news. He jumped off the horse and climbed the few steps, two at a time towards the main door. He didn't wait for anyone to come. Instead he threw the door wide open and began to shout. 'Lady Mackintosh! Lady Mackintosh! I have news for you! Urgent news!'

When one of the servants came from the kitchen, he pushed him aside. 'I must speak to Lady Mackintosh. It's urgent. I have news.'

A number of people came to see what all the fuss was about, but Ian Og continued to call for Her Ladyship and after a few minutes she arrived, a cloak gathered around her night attire. Soon a young man, also in night attire but of a richer fabric than usual, came to see what all the shouting was about. He had fair curly hair and blue eyes, and he looked at Ian Og whom he recognised.

'I have news, madam. I have important news.'

'You can tell my staff.'

'No, madam. It's for your ears only. It came from Forbes. I have just come from there.'

At this information, she nodded to the man beside her, and said to Ian Og, 'Speak no more here. You may join us in the side room.'

She led the way. Within the little room, Ian Og stood silent until the two were seated and Lady Mackintosh looked up at him and said, 'Now, tell us what news you bring that is so important.'

Knowing that the young man seated beside her was indeed the prince he'd met before at Blair Castle, Ian Og took a couple of deep breaths to calm himself before speaking of the impending raid. 'Alistair Glic was present in the Forbes' kitchen when the servants were talking about expecting government soldiers from Inverness. Their target was this estate and the prince, whom they hope to capture tomorrow.'

'Tomorrow? You're sure?' asked a startled Lady MacKintosh.

'It might just be gossip, madam, but Alistair was disguised as a foolish English soldier with no knowledge of Gaelic, and the staff didn't know he could understand every word.'

'Why didn't he come himself?'

'He has gathered some important information from a courier, and he must get it to Keppoch and Locheil as soon as possible.' He paused. 'He doesn't think the raid is gossip, and it would be foolish to ignore it.'

'Yes indeed,' she said as she rose. 'Get yourself something to eat and come when I call for the men to assist.'

As Ian Og left the room he heard her speak to the prince. 'You will have to leave us for the night, sire.'

Daylight was still an hour away when Ian Og, asleep with his head resting on the kitchen table, awoke to the call for assistance.

In the main room all the available men of the estate were gathered. There only nine and two of these were on crutches. Angus was there, and clearly surprised to see Ian Og.

The tacksman had a plan. It required the men to give the impression that they were part of a large defending force. They were to be stationed out of sight, behind the hayshed and in the trees, within range of the track. The men on crutches would be stationary in different places and shout fake orders to non-existent defenders while the rest would move about.

Lady MacKintosh took Angus to one side, and after a few minutes, she beckoned to Ian Og. 'You are clearly a loyal young man, and Angus here says you are also intelligent and resourceful. You will therefore go with him and take the prince to a safe place that no one here, not even I, may know, in case we are overrun.'

Shortly afterwards, three riders left the estate, slowly ambling south towards one of the old drove roads. Angus pointed out to the prince that any observer would expect fugitives to be galloping in haste, so their unhurried pace would lull any suspicion.

In a small clearing at the edge of the estate there was a derelict-looking shed. Angus prised open the doors and led the way. Inside there was enough room to hide the three riders and their horses. It was the site of one of Angus's old stills. In his absence, it hadn't been used for some time, but hidden inside was all the equipment needed for distilling, and also several dusty old flagons.

Angus sighed with satisfaction, remembering days gone by. From his sporran he brought out his horn and filled it from one of the flagons. The prince was given the first taste. He took a generous mouthful, and then spluttered and coughed and handed it back to Angus. Ian Og brought his own horn from his sporran and handed it to Angus. It was filled and returned. Unlike the prince, Ian Og knew to take a gentle sip at first, to assess how strong the potion was, but he too found himself coughing at its undiluted strength. Soon, weariness overcame him and he settled down to rest on the ground near the horses, and fell asleep while the others talked.

The prince carefully continued to sip the whisky and began to ask Angus about life in the Highlands, and the government troops. Most of it was in Gaelic, but from time to time the prince reverted to his native French. Fortunately, Angus was able to reply and whenever Ian Og was aroused from his sleep, he was pleased he could understand quite a lot of their words.

Back at Moy Hall, it was with the light of dawn when the soldiers tasked with the capture of Bonnie Prince Charlie arrived. They had marched all night, and now they spread out quietly, creeping under the cover of the trees that surrounded the estate, hoping to have the element of surprise.

They were not expecting a strong military voice, calling out, 'Aim ... Fire!' and what sounded like a volley of shots coming towards them. Two soldiers were killed immediately. Quickly they moved sideways but another voice could be heard saying 'Steady, men ... Steady ... Pick your targets.' This happened a few times, and more of the soldiers were killed by this hidden enemy. Soon the attackers decided they were up against superior numbers and withdrew. It was obvious they had been expected.

The defenders waited at their posts until they were certain that there would be no counter-attack. One of the fittest men followed them on foot, dodging from tree to bush to rock to stay under cover. He wanted to make sure the troops were heading back towards Inverness.

When Lady Mackintosh got confirmation the troops had gone, she invited the whole estate back to the hall to drink the health of the prince, and ordered that three single gunshots be fired from the hall.

Down in the shed, having heard the shots, Angus, the prince, and Ian Og knew all was clear, and with a final dram of whisky the three mounted up and went to join the celebrations. Ian Og's news had saved the prince but he had missed all the action fighting the soldiers. There would be another day for that, he hoped.

Later that day, Ian Og was reluctant to be on his way home, but Angus pointed out that Anghie was expecting a load of grain for the still. The grain would also be a great help to fill stomachs as well as make whisky. The family needed any siller the whisky could bring them. Ian Og, with a loaded packhorse, reluctantly left Moy Hall in the afternoon of that eventful day and made his way home.

CHAPTER 18

IT WAS LATE EVENING when Alistair arrived at Keppoch Castle. With an attentive group of uncles and cousins to hear what news he brought, he was sat at the table beside the fire. Warm broth, bannock and a dram were laid before him. He supped hungrily while he read the notes he took from Torquil MacLeod's precious letters.

While he went through the catalogue of Jacobite friends and foes, the men nodded and frowned in turn, making comments to each other. Before Alistair finished, his audience was already deep in discussion on their next moves for the prince.

Soon he was alone. He folded his arms on the table, rested his head and sleep overwhelmed him. Mrs Cameron, the housekeeper, soon returned and saw him there, dead to the world. Gently she draped a hide over him.

When eventually he awoke, it was daylight and all was quiet. He was thirsty, so he rose stiffly and went to find some ale or water. As he made his way through the kitchen towards the pump outside, he noticed a large jug of ale on a shelf. Eagerly he gulped it down. Only then did he take a look around him. He could see that the house was almost empty. His news had obviously been important enough to send the clan scrambling into action. He hoped Ian Og had arrived in time to warn the prince of the impending danger.

There were pots around the embers of the fire and he found some tired porridge. He gathered it up with other scraps left on the table, stirred them together with sour milk and made himself a breakfast that would see him through the day. Mrs Cameron heard him moving. She bustled in with a jug of fresh milk for him, and when she sat down, began to ask after Sarah and the other children in Glen Rowan. 'She's a fine lass that one and I hope the little ones are all well. It must be difficult for her now with the men away. You're keeping an eye on them, I hope.'

Alistair wasn't really listening, but nodded or shook his head whenever it seemed the right thing to do.

While he ate, she told him that some of the men had gone to help at Moy Hall, if it was necessary, and others to see Cameron of Locheil in Glen Nevis, where he was asked to go when he woke. The clansmen were preparing to head up to Inverness because there was news that Cumberland and his army were heading north up the east coast. Fort Augustus had fallen, which was good news for the Jacobites, but no doubt some of the soldiers would head to what they hoped would be safety at Fort William. All the local clansmen were called to assist one of the Jacobite army leaders, Colonel Grant, who was preparing to lay siege to the fort, in the hope of getting their surrender.

Mrs Cameron prattled on. 'I won't get a chance to see her today, but tomorrow I'll send more food up to Sarah, and let her know you and Hamish got back safely. She'll want to know what happened to Ian Og. What can I tell her?'

'Just that he went to warn Lady Mackintosh and there was likely to be some trouble. When I was in Forbes' kitchen I learned they knew the prince was hiding at Moy Hall and they had a plan to capture him there.'

It wasn't long before Alistair was on his way, and he made good time to catch up with Locheil at Glen Nevis. He was asked to go down to Maryburgh and assist Colonel Grant. Although it was quiet when he reached the wee town, a large part of it was within range of the fort so he went carefully around and was soon at the Craigs, a small stony outcrop not visible to the soldiers.

Colonel Grant and his lieutenants were in discussion, planning the best site for the guns to do most damage to the fort.

'Alistair, the very man!' exclaimed the colonel. 'Fort Augustus has cracked and the Royal-Ecossais troops are on their way here to assist us. I've also sent a messenger down to Corran, telling them to bring their cannons. I am determined to have a swift and mighty barrage of the fort. We'll need all the firepower we can lay our hands on to get rid of that evil Commander Scott, before we finish and head towards Inverness and face Cumberland's army. The prince and his army are up near Inverness. They're trying to keep the coast open for French reinforcements and artillery that's on its way. It would be great to get the help from the French. Make things a lot easier.'

Alistair smiled. Had the prince been captured, all Scotland would know by now. Ian Og had obviously been successful in his mission.

'We've not been having much luck here, but with a bit more firepower tonight, I'm going to send a messenger to them with an offer to cease fire if they surrender. Get yourself some rest and join us in the morning.'

A few minutes later, remembering his promise to keep Hamish informed, Alistair cautiously threaded his way through a somewhat scarred Maryburgh and knocked at the door of his house. It was a relief that it wasn't the formidable Lizzie who answered. Hamish appeared and with a slight nod of his head, indicated there was company and stepped outside to hear the news Alistair carried.

'I can't stop for long, Hamish. I thought you might like to know that Mrs Cameron, the housekeeper of Keppoch Castle, is keeping a friendly eye on Sarah and the family up in the glen. So they should be all right for a while. The colonel wants me on standby for tomorrow. So I just called to let you know that the "kestrel" we were talking about,' he paused to make sure Hamish remembered their code for a siege of the fort before continuing, '… looks likely and fairly soon.'

'In the meantime, I'm heading off to the forge to get my horse shod. It will be a warm place to rest my head for a while.'

'Thanks for letting me know,' said Hamish with a smiling nod to show he had understood the message.

It was the next morning when a refreshed Alistair and his newly shod horse arrived back at the Craigs to rejoin Colonel Grant and his men. He found that the Royal-Ecossais and the cannons had arrived. There was plenty of chat in Gaelic, Scots, broken English and French. Over the weeks, the gunners had grown familiar with each other. Few were fluent in Gaelic, but all managed to catch up with news and gossip while they prepared their meals. Alistair joined them.

Colonel Grant was already directing the barrage of Fort William. The men were rested and had food inside them, and they set to work with renewed vigour. The range was somewhat further than they would have wished, but the target was large enough. The success up at Fort Augustus in Kilcumin was boosting everyone's confidence. One or two could be heard whistling cheerfully while they piled up mortars, and made sure the guns were ready to shoot again and again.

As they worked, the men continued to chat, not always about the task in hand.

'So, did she have a girl or a boy?'

'A lovely wee boy. After the three girls, I thought it would never happen. They're awful small, aren't they? I was really glad to get home to see them.'

'You were lucky that Augustus didn't take long.'

'Yes, it wasn't very well put together so when we hit the weakest part, the rest sort of disintegrated. The new road's good too, and when Grant said we could take a rest, it didn't take me long to get home.'

'Then, when I got back later, Grant made sure that we got some decent provisions brought down from Inverness. So with the supplies we also took from Augustus, we can last for a while.'

'Yeah, Grant is a decent sort of man.'

'Some of them are bastards. Get a man flogged for looking in the wrong direction. It's no way to run a war. One of the local subalterns managed to really annoy his men, and the next day there were none of them left; slipped off in the night to see how their families were coping. Don't know if they ever came back. I don't think I would.'

As they worked, the men shared whisky, brandy, ale and rations. Others were catching up with the news from Inverness while they set up the furnace ready to forge new cannonballs.

The gunners were experienced soldiers, and included some Irish and a number of French mercenaries. Most took the chance of a catnap around midday but they were up and ready again in the early afternoon when Colonel Grant announced it was time to 'show them again we mean business.' He nodded to the bugle boy. At the first note, there was a deafening roar and the cannons resumed their fire.

Meanwhile, up in the glen, Anghie came running in. 'Sarah! Sarah! It's Ian Og. He's coming up the track and it looks as if he's got a load of grain on a packhorse.'

'What a relief!' Sarah paused in the middle of plucking a chicken, which was a very welcome gift, brought over from Keppoch by Mrs Cameron herself. She quickly wiped her hands and ran to the door to give a hearty welcome to her brother.

'Thank God you're safe!'

She hugged him and brought him into the warm croft as Anghie took charge of the horses and the grain they carried.

'Mrs Cameron said you went to Moy Hall to save the prince, but that Alistair hadn't seen you since then and didn't know how you got on.' She poured ale into a bowl for him and resumed plucking the chicken.

'Alistair doesn't know. I haven't seen him since I set out to alert the prince.'

Having unloaded the grain up at the still, Anghie joined them, keen to know what had happened.

Ian Og took a deep sup of the ale and then continued,

more excitedly each moment, as he relayed the details. It was obvious that he was only now realising how important the role he played in the last twenty-four hours had been to the prince and the Jacobite cause.

'Alistair told us what he heard in Forbes' kitchen, that there was a plot to capture the prince. He and Hamish had to get back here, so I was the one selected to go and tell Lady Mackintosh about it. The prince, too, he was there. I was awestruck!'

Sarah and Anghie were hanging on his every word.

'The prince was there?' said Anghie.

'Yes ... Lady Mackintosh brought me into a private room because she was aware we had to be cautious. I had told her my news concerned the prince and it was for her ears only. Of course, the prince too.'

'Later, when she called everyone to the hall, Angus was there. I couldn't believe it at first, but of course he spent a lot of time there when he was young.'

'The tacksman had a scheme to fool any soldiers they might send to capture the prince. He began to organise this with the estate folk, but Lady Mackintosh had a different job for us. She knows Angus well and trusts him, and as my uncle, he vouched for me. So she gave us some food and charged the two of us with keeping His Highness safe. Her husband is on the side of the Hanoverians, so she presumed it was one of the estate folk who alerted the authorities.'

'What did ye do?' asked Sarah in a concerned voice.

'Angus knows all the nooks and crannies that the gaugers haven't found, and he has plenty of hiding places for his whisky. So, we went to one of his special places. You should have seen it. Honestly, Sarah, Angus was ready for almost any emergency. Dried meat hanging there out of sight, and dried carrots, kale and other stuff, still good to eat. We hardly needed Lady Mackintosh's fresh food!'

'What did ye talk about with the prince? Could you understand him?' asked Sarah.

'We talked about everything. Angus turned out to be very good at the French language and got on very well with the prince. I was pleased I'd had those French lessons with the dominie and I began to talk with him a bit as well. But he was very good at the Gaelic too, and said he recognised me from when I got his gold button. I don't know if he meant it, but he said it would be an *honour* to visit us in Glen Rowan when the fighting is over.'

'Oh … imagine! That would be wonderful. So, Angus is still with him?'

'I think so, but I'm not sure. When we knew it was safe, we all went back to Moy Hall. The prince was heading off to catch up with the army coming north from Falkirk and Angus felt he must go with him for the time being. He told me to stay at Moy Hall and collect a load of grain and bring it up here for Anghie.'

'I heard that the army was back in Scotland because yon English folk wouldn't join them. Can you believe that?' said Anghie. 'We have a duty to show them all that God is on our side with the anointed King's son.'

'Aye,' agreed Ian Og, 'but sometimes you wouldn't think it.' He looked around at the youngsters now gathered in front of the fire. 'And what's been happening here?'

'All the local men went away, and although quite a few of them came back to get some crops into the ground, we had to do most of that ourselves,' said Sarah. 'But Anghie was great. He'd rather be off with the prince, but knows we couldn't manage without him.'

She smiled and nodded at Anghie who was looking a bit bashful at the praise. 'He gets the wee kids to help him. You can hear them singing as they are doing it. It's been a hard time, but plenty of good moments. Mrs Cameron down at Keppoch keeps an eye on us too. She's been very kind. Helps with a bit of food now and again. Sent us this chicken. It's good to get some fresh meat inside us, now and again.'

As the youngsters pottered around them, the three gossiped about the local news, the recent fall of Fort Augustus and the new siege of Fort William.

'Yes,' said Ian Og. 'I heard about that.' He stood up. 'I think I ought to be heading down there to assist. Anything to get rid of these Hanoverians.'

'Alistair is probably there,' said Sarah rising. 'He was heading there after he'd passed on his information to the folk at Keppoch. We haven't heard much about it one way or another since then.'

Ian Og gathered up his belongings. Anghie rose with a great yawn and went to check on the horses. Sarah also stood up and hugged Ian Og. 'You take care of yourself and may God keep us all well.'

'Are you OK, Sarah?' Ian Og had noticed that there was something different about his sister, but he could not make out what it was.

'Yes, Ian Og. I'm fine. Just a bit stressed with all the worry.' Sarah knew that now was not the time to tell Ian Og she was pregnant.

Night was falling when Sarah, Anghie and the youngsters waved goodbye to Ian Og as he made his way down the hill.

In the meantime, down at the Craigs that evening, Alistair, being Grant's link with Keppoch and Locheil, listened to a heated discussion among the officers. Everyone was very disappointed with the poor results for the day's efforts, and eventually decided to bring the cannons a hundred yards closer to the target during the night.

Unfortunately, this meant that the attackers were not only closer to the fort, but they were closer to snipers. The colonel's gunners did their work, but the defenders kept up a dangerous random fire. Two men were killed and Colonel Grant himself suffered a shot that broke his leg. Alistair, being the local man, took him to the healer Conn Orchy, who lived on the Achintore road. While Alistair held the wounded colonel, he learned colourful words in several foreign languages. Fortunately, it didn't take long before the leg was back in shape. With herbs and splints to keep his leg straight and with a large dram inside him, the colonel insisted he was well enough and must return to his post.

At the officers' meeting later that evening, it was felt it might be a good time to seek the fort's surrender. They all turned to look at Alistair. As he was Keppoch's nephew rather than a soldier, they reckoned he would be the best person for the task. The following morning, riding the colonel's own white charger and bearing the Jacobite standard, Alistair, wearing full Highland dress obtained from a local cousin and led in by a French drummer lad, approached the fort to offer the soldiers there safe passage if they surrendered.

CHAPTER 19

WHEN IAN OG REACHED Maryburgh, he made his way to Hamish's house. Cautiously, he tapped at the door and was relieved when Hamish himself answered. Hamish told him that Lizzie was not there and invited him in.

With a bowl of ale now in front of him and a warm fire burning in the hearth, Ian Og enthusiastically told Hamish of his time with the prince in Moy Hall. He also told him of their concealment of the prince in one of Angus's old whisky hideouts. He was particularly pleased that although the prince spoke Gaelic, his own French worked quite well over the few days they were together.

Gradually the talk moved to the news in the town. Ian Og was disappointed to learn that Colonel Grant's gunners hadn't succeeded in getting the fort to surrender. The previous day they'd made a non-stop barrage with their cannons.

'We were almost deafened by it,' said Hamish. 'Went on all day. I doubt there's a complete roof or wall left in the fort. Alistair was sent with the French drummer lad to offer them all safe passage if they were to leave immediately.' He began to laugh. 'I'm not sure what Commander Scott said, but it sounds as if he was hopping mad and sent him off with a flea in his ear. I don't think they're likely to give up any time soon.'

'Quite a few of the redcoats are already on the march to Inverness. Word is that Cumberland's army is heading north from Aberdeen, so it's likely there will be some action there. Mammy's friend David and his regiment are going to join them.' Hamish sighed. 'She's very sad about it. They were getting on very well, and she was becoming a different person, much happier. So I'll be taking her over to the fort tomorrow to say goodbye.' He sighed again. 'It was good while it lasted.'

Ian Og didn't want make any remarks about Lizzie and felt it might be helpful to change the subject. 'So ... where can I find Alistair, do you know?'

'Yes. Someone told me he got fed up with the whole lot of them at the Craigs yesterday. He was annoyed they had chosen him to go to the fort with the drummer rather than one of their own men. Seems he reported straight back to Grant and then headed up the Cow Hill to get away.'

'Oh, that's handy,' said Ian Og. 'I'll catch up with him up there and tell him all about Moy Hall.' He swallowed down the last of his ale and stood up. 'Thanks, Hamish. I'd better go. I'll be up there for tonight and aim to see you tomorrow after I report to Grant. Lord knows what's going to happen, but it's pretty messy, isn't it?' At the door, he clasped his friend's hand and said, 'Good luck with your mother.'

It didn't take long to reach the gunners on the Cow Hill. As expected, Alistair was there and everyone was chatting about the day's events. Ian Og settled his horse and joined them beside the fire.

Alistair had been in a black mood since his visit to the fort that morning, but was cheered to hear what was happening up in the glen. The two friends chatted happily about the family, particularly Sarah. 'She's getting a little tummy on her now, isn't she?' said a smiling Alistair.

'Yes, I noticed that,' said Ian Og. 'It is not as if she is eating a lot.'

A bemused Alistair laughed at Ian Og's naivety. 'It's nothing to do with eating.'

'Well, what's it got to do with?'

'Don't you know?'

'Know what?'

'She's with child. You're going to be an uncle, Ian Og.'

'What? Does Hamish know?'

'I don't know. I guess he must.'

'Well,' said Ian Og. 'I was with him earlier today and he never said anything to me about being an uncle, so he mustn't know yet.'

'Oh dear,' said Alistair. 'You mustn't tell anyone else. I am sure Sarah is looking for the right moment to tell him and you about it. I should have kept my big mouth shut.'

'Don't worry. I won't say anything.' Then with a touch of pride in his voice added, 'I'm going to be an uncle – me!'

'But first we have to win this war, Ian Og. Not just for Bonnie Prince Charlie and Scotland, but for all the generations to come.'

Ian Og then told of his adventure with the prince. Alistair and the gunners who had joined them were all ears. Gradually, the embers of the fire faded, and the company settled down to rest. Soon the two friends were fast asleep, quite heedless of the wind around them and the war they were engaged in.

Back at Fort William, however, a very angry Commander Scott had taken the message from the Jacobites personally. It was an insult that he should ever consider yielding his command under such an irritating and ineffectual barrage. He gathered together his officers and formulated a plan to raid the enemy, damage the guns and take some prisoners. That would show he was not a man to be trifled with.

Just after dawn the next day, two raiding parties quietly left the fort for the Craigs and Cow Hill. It was unfortunate for Ian Og and Alistair that they were the first to be kicked awake and guns put to their heads, while the rest of the company grabbed whatever was near them and made their escape. The two watched the mortars being spiked, damaged beyond any further assault, and within minutes found themselves roped together, hemmed in by redcoats, being marched back to Fort William with a few other stragglers.

Neither saw Lizzie at the gate waving goodbye to David, her redcoat friend, before he marched off towards Inverness. But she saw the exuberant soldiers arrive, parading their captives, including Alistair and Ian Og, prodding them like cattle. She drew back within the shadow of the wall to watch what was happening.

It was unfortunate that Torquil MacLeod, who was again on his way to Lord President Forbes at Culloden, called to the fort that morning with letters for Commander Scott. When he saw the unlucky prisoners, he had no difficulty recognising the pathetic 'Lieutenant

Corbet' and one of his accomplices who together had ransacked his precious letters. Almost speechless with anger, he approached the nearest officer to tell him that these two were rebel spies for the Jacobite cause.

The subaltern seemed very pleased with MacLeod's intervention.

'Many thanks, sir.' He bowed his head. 'These are difficult times and we must be careful with these rebels. I shall take charge of them myself and make sure they do not escape retribution for their wrongdoings.' He signalled that these two prisoners should walk ahead of him and said, 'I wish that others were as observant and loyal as you are. These two will serve their punishment when I take them to one of the ships now upping anchor and taking other prisoners to work on the plantations in the Americas. His Majesty thanks you.'

Lizzie observed the whole incident. She shrank further back into the shadows and watched as the prisoners and subaltern headed along the jetty towards the sailing ships. She saw them pause. The subaltern was obviously questioning them but she would never have guessed what was being said.

'It's Alistair and Ian Og, isn't it?'

'Gosh!' said Ian Og, looking more carefully. 'It's Peter! How are you? What a change in five years. And you're speaking the Gaelic too.'

'Oh yes. After our adventure together five years ago I knew the Gaelic would come in handy. I was hoping to catch up with you sometime. But not like this.'

Alistair nodded in agreement. 'Yes, it's not the best time for us three to meet again.'

'That's true,' Peter sighed. 'And unlucky too that MacLeod saw you. You certainly upset him. He has always been a bit of a pest. Said you two were spies and I ought to take you to the commander. Lucky he didn't see you yesterday when you came all dressed up.'

'Ah, don't remind me,' Alistair sadly shook his head. 'And when your commander sees me, I'll get strung up straight away.'

'Well, I have an idea. It might get us all out of a jam. My time to pay the debt I owe you, but you may prefer to face Commander Scott.'

'Oh no, thank you, Peter! We know about him. Don't we, Ian Og? So let's hear what you suggest. The soldiers will soon realise we haven't come back, and MacLeod is bound to ask. We wouldn't want you to get into any trouble.'

Peter smiled. 'There are a couple of ships heading out. Frigates from Glasgow. They're heading for the Americas with supplies, and have been collecting prisoners to work on the plantations.' He pointed to the ships, both now dressed with sails. 'Should just about be ready to cast off. I was talking with some of the crewmen when they came ashore four days ago, and yesterday one said they were several men short. I could add you to their list. I can say you'd be no trouble and would be safe to help the crew rather than spending time below with the others. It may not be what you would ever choose for yourself but it would be better than Commander Scott and a hanging.'

Walking towards the waiting ship, they chatted about Sarah, Uncle Angus and how the family were faring in these troubled times. Truthfully, Alistair and Ian Og were able to say they didn't know where Angus was nor who he might be with, but told Peter that Sarah was now betrothed to Hamish.

'Aye, these are strange times,' Peter sighed. 'I fear I

shall be sent with the men to Inverness tomorrow. In the meantime, it is time to make a decision.'

Alistair sucked in his breath. 'Hanging or the American plantations.' He closed his eyes for a moment and saw in his mind the curve of Sarah's dark eyebrows, her rosy cheeks flushed from exertion, the earnest brown eyes, and the thought that he might never see her again wrung his heart.

'Yes, the Americas,' he said after a few moments. 'I can't say it is much of a choice, but we're caught between a rock and a hard place. Anything other than execution.'

Ian Og quickly nodded his agreement.

'Come with me,' said Peter, 'and I'll speak to the crewmen.'

It took a few minutes to walk to the ship where sailors were loading the last of the supplies. Peter spoke quietly to the sailor on guard. One ship had already cast off from the pier and this was the last one.

Down by the gate, Lizzie watched the three of them. She saw the subaltern speak to the sailor at the gangplank and point to the two prisoners. Quickly she turned and hastened away from the fort. She met Hamish heading towards the fort.

'Let's get away quick, Hamish. We don't want anyone to see you. You're one of their friends.' She began to pull him away.

'Why? What's happening?'

'I'll tell you when we're away from here. Let's get away, quick.'

Back at home, Hamish found it difficult to piece together what his mother was saying. At last, he realised that someone made it known to one of the officers that

Alistair and Ian Og were rebel spies and Lizzie had seen them board a ship bound for the plantations in the Americas.

'So who spoke to the officer? Do you know him? What did he look like?'

Although Lizzie was upset, she tried to remember what the informer looked like. Gradually from her comments Hamish realised who it was. 'Was he wearing MacLeod tartan?'

'Yes, yes, that's it! Who is he?'

'Sounds like Torquil MacLeod. Oh dear … at least they are alive, and the American plantations are a better choice than a hanging or a shooting here. I'd better go back tomorrow and see what I can find out.'

CHAPTER 20

THE FOLLOWING MORNING after a troubled night, Hamish went to the gates of Fort William determined to find out what had happened to Alistair and Ian Og. He invented a plausible excuse for the gateman, and tried to sound business like as he asked, 'Were there any prisoners left in the cells? Or perhaps any hangings overnight?'

Although the gatemen knew Hamish, they were cautious with all visitors in these troubled times, so he wasn't let in. Not to be daunted, he tried to sound nonchalant.

'It's Skeegan Cameron. I'm just checking for his mother, because he hasn't been seen for days. We thought you might have him.'

The gatemen were happy to gossip. 'No. We haven't seen him for ages. He is always getting drunk, and setting fire to things. Then he'd say he'd seen a fire and come to help us put it out.'

'So you didn't have anyone at all in the cells yesterday?'

'Well, we do have Duncan MacPherson, but you

couldn't call him much of a prisoner, could you? Another pesky local. So drunk last night when he turned up at the fort, he could hardly stand, insisting he was the head man on the Highland clans' war council! He said he came to negotiate peace between us all. Good job Commander Scott didn't see him. He'd have been strung up straight away. He's feeling terrible now and it'll be an hour or two before he's fit enough to be thrown out the back gate. No doubt, like everyone else, soldiers or clansmen, he'll head for Inverness. Bonnie Charlie is up there somewhere and I reckon there is going to be a lot of bloodshed. I won't be sorry to miss it.'

This didn't quite answer Hamish's concerns. 'Your sergeant wouldn't have any paperwork about other prisoners, would he? Mrs Cameron is really very anxious.'

'Well ... I'll take a look for you. Wait here.'

On his return, the man said there was no sign of Skeegan, and apart from drunken Duncan, only a few other prisoners were listed: some Cameron clansman taken from the Craigs, and after being questioned they were let go. Everyone, whether Hanoverian Government, Jacobite clansman, French Royal-Ecossais or a local drunk, was no longer a concern for the fort. All were heading, by different routes, towards Inverness. The siege of the fort was over.

A baffled Hamish made his way home. 'God bless all here,' he said as usual when entering the house, but was surprised to find Lizzie gathering some of her belongings into a bundle on the table.

'What's happening, Mammy?'

As she continued to tidy her bundle, Lizzie sighed. 'I don't want to be here, Hamish. Everyone has gone. I now realise my old life is gone too, and I feel that David is where my life lies. So I'm going to take this chance to catch up with him on the road to Inverness. Who knows what may happen, but I have to go. He's such a good man, I would be foolish to let him slip though my fingers just because I still feel I ought to protect your dad's memory.'

'Oh Mammy, with all this fighting ahead of us, just go! Take the chance while you have it. You've been good to us. We're all grown up now. It's your turn to have your own life with somebody you like. David is a decent man. I'd be pleased to know you were with him in these strange times and I know the girls will be happy for you as well.'

'I can take you up to the junction of the military roads beside Fort Augustus myself tomorrow, and with two of us keeping an eye out for David, it shouldn't take long. But today, I have to get up to the glen and make sure Sarah and the rest are okay. I have to let her know that you watched Ian Og and Alistair being put on one of those ships heading out for the plantations in America. It's not the best news, but at least she won't be worrying that they are already dead or will get killed in any of the fighting we're going to face when Cumberland turns up.'

Hamish looked around. 'Tomorrow, I ought to get to the forge and tell them I won't be there for a while. With everyone heading for Inverness they'll probably know already, but I need to tell them myself. It won't take long, but I don't want to keep you waiting more than I have to, and although it's unlikely, if they have any spare horses I'll get one for you. It'll be quite a long journey to Dornoch or wherever you're going.'

Lizzie came close to her son, put her arms around his shoulders and gave him a kiss on each cheek. 'Thank you, Hamish. I'm happy to wait for you here and I can say my farewells to the neighbours.' She began to clear some of the shelves. 'Now, I'll get some food together for our own journey and you can take the rest to Sarah. It'll be tough for them up there and I wouldn't like her to go hungry.'

A couple of hours later, Hamish with laden horse arrived in the glen. Anghie, the girls and wee Jimmy were always on watch for visitors, so Sarah soon learned of his coming and was waiting at the door to greet him. Even before Hamish dismounted, Anghie was unloading the precious cargo and giving most of it to the youngsters to be hidden away from prying eyes.

For Hamish, it was a joy to see his precious Sarah. He embraced her, gave her Lizzie's good wishes and asked how she was.

'I have news for you, Hamish, but first tell me what you know about the siege of Fort William. Did you see Ian Og or Alistair?'

Ale was poured and while he slaked his thirst, he told her of the capture of Alistair and Ian Og. He said his mother watched as they were escorted on to a ship bound for the plantations in America. The news was not of great comfort to her, but they both agreed that life on the American plantations was a better result than the hanging they would have surely faced with Commander Scott. One day they would find a way to return home.

As the evening grew darker, the young ones gradually settled into their bed spaces near the hearth and its waning fire. Sarah brought Hamish through into the backroom where they lay close together on Grannie's old bed.

'You said you had news for me, Sarah?'

Taking his hand and laying it on her belly, she whispered. 'Can you feel it moving, Hamish?'

'Sarah!' he exclaimed excitedly. 'You're pregnant.'

'Yes, had you no idea? Did you not notice I was getting fatter lately?'

'No, Sarah. With all the events recently and all the comings and goings I was too busy to notice. I'm sorry.'

'What are we going to do, Hamish?'

'Don't worry, Sarah. I'll look after you and the baby.'

As he held her closely, Sarah was silent for a moment. She hoped that Hamish indeed was the father of her child but she wasn't sure.

'You are my family now, Sarah,' said Hamish. 'My mother is going to Inverness to be with the man she loves, my sisters are in domestic service and I will provide for you and our baby. The little ones too, of course.'

'Hamish, you're such a good man.'

They talked until gradually each slipped into sleep.

Dawn had hardly appeared before the young ones were rising and going about their daily tasks. In kindness they didn't intend to disturb Sarah and Hamish, but a clatter of pails returning from the well and logs being laid beside the hearth soon dragged the two from sleep and into the main room.

Anghie was making the porridge while the girls milked the goat. The breakfast set before Hamish as he sat at the table was almost lavish. Although he was hungry, he didn't want to deprive anyone of their own food, so he took just a spoonful or two before saying he must get back to his mother as soon as possible.

The youngsters, keen to help, fetched and saddled his horse while he gathered what he needed. A parting embrace and kiss with Sarah, and soon horse and rider were trotting back down the glen.

On reaching Maryburgh, Hamish made his way to the forge. It was cold. The fire was out. Neither Smith Cameron nor his son were there, and sadly, no horse for Lizzie. There were words scratched on the anvil saying, 'We'll bring them back.' Hamish read these words over and over. What could they mean? Who had written this message and was it for him or the smith? Clearly, others were leaving Fort William, and didn't want to walk. Why would they leave a message without a name? Disappointed, he headed home, but he could not get the words out of his mind. They meant something but he wasn't sure what.

He found his mother sitting quietly in front of the fading ashes of the hearth fire, and looking at an untidy earthy lump on the floor. As she rose to put bannocks and ale on the table, she pointed down to the messy bundle and handed him a knife.

'It's been thirty years so I don't know how well it has survived, but I think you can probably make good use of it.'

Bemused, Hamish made a cut on the tattered lump. It seemed like a very ancient dirty oily sheepskin and his curiosity was aroused. It took quite a few stabs before he began to realise what might be hiding there. Triumphantly, he lifted out a mucky old broadsword.

Lizzie scratched at it and went to find a rasp. She handed the rasp to her son, saying, 'You'll need some work to get it cleaned and honed, but it should still be a good sword, Hamish. It was my father's. When he died after Sherrifmuir thirty years ago, I buried it because I wanted to save it for my future son. Granny Morag did the same. We buried our men's swords but we never got to bury our men. Ian Og has his grandpa's sword and now this is yours.'

'I will always treasure it, Mother. Thank you for looking after it.'

Eagerly taking the rasp, Hamish began to remove the dirt and rust of three decades and after a few minutes was suddenly surprised by his mother tapping him on his shoulder.

'God bless you, Hamish. We'll take some food but we'd better get a move on or I'll never catch up with David. You've always been a good son to me and when … if … he and I make a home together, I will always be grateful to you who made it possible.' She raised her bowl of ale and stood to drink to it. 'To a new life for us both.'

'To a new life for us all, including my baby,' replied Hamish.

'Sarah's pregnant? That's wonderful news, Hamish,' exclaimed Lizzie. 'I'm going to be a grandmother.'

With that she raised her mug again. 'To a new life for us all!'

'Slainte!' said Hamish in agreement.

Soon he was mounted with Lizzie sitting sideways behind him, a fond arm around his waist as the horse made its way steadily along General Wade's fine road. It wasn't long before they caught up with some soldiers. As they passed more soldiers along the road, Lizzie cast her eyes over those they met along the way. Hamish kept the horse steady on its path, not daring to look sideways. He was tense until, with a sturdy grasp on his arm, Lizzie spoke quietly into his ear.

'There he is, Hamish, there he is.' She was already slipping off his horse and gathering her bundle.

Quickly, Hamish too dismounted, just in time to throw his arms around her and say, 'God keep you, Mammy.' For a few moments, he watched as she greeted David, then he smiled, remounted and waved at the pair before turning the horse towards the old road, heading back to Sarah and the family in Glen Rowan.

It was unfortunate that within a few minutes he met up with a cheery band of MacDonell clansmen from Glen Spean. They greeted him happily and when he said he was heading up to Glen Rowan to see Sarah, they scoffed and took a grip of his reins.

'You'll miss it all. Everyone is heading for Inverness. We've got the whole countryside heading there to give that man Cumberland a good thrashing. That's what your Sarah would like to hear when we all march home again.'

'But I've only got an old rusty sword and a wee knife. It's hardly enough to go into battle. I must get up to the glen and get my shield.'

'No worries then.' The men were cheerfully intoxicated. 'We've been gathering up all sorts of hidden weapons in the glens.' One of them beckoned another in the group. 'Duncan, you've got that extra shield, haven't you?' When the lad nodded, he continued, 'You've only got two hands, so give the spare one to Hamish and he won't need to get back to his glen.'

CHAPTER 21

THE HIGHLAND GREAT GLEN has a line of lochs which cut through mighty mountains from Inverness, past Fort Augustus, to Fort William and onward to the rocky Corran Narrows, where rushing waters escape westwards, passing rocky islands till they flow into the Atlantic Ocean.

Dadda, Roderick and Ranald had been at Corran for many days, assisting with the cannons. Several government ships had already come to grief trying to slip through the narrows; two had been sunk with all hands lost. The gunners were in high spirits, so it was a bit disappointing when a rider came with orders from Colonel Grant besieging Fort William that all the guns and gunners were to make haste towards Inverness. Cumberland's army was making its way north from Aberdeen and every mortar and cannon was needed to stop his advance.

Although disappointed to leave possible further triumphs at the Corran waters, the men gathered their equipment and began to head towards the more important challenges at Inverness.

Dadda, Roderick and Ranald were with the last of the gunners getting their cannon ready for the long march, when Ranald saw a ship making its way into the narrows. He yelled and everyone looked back, stopped and watched. Only government ships passed these days.

Looking at Dadda, an eager Ranald asked, 'Can we have one last shot before we go? We saw them heading up to the fort a week ago and this is going to be the last one we see for a while. Let's sink it, shall we?'

'Yes!' Dadda nodded complete agreement with his gentle brother. 'I would really like to stop them in their tracks. One last try and then we will have to go. It would send us to Inverness with a great victory behind us.'

The two gunners had already dragged the cannon into position. Swiftly the men brought forward their last three cannonballs and reopened the gunpowder cask. The cannon was loaded with powder, the ball added and the cannon sergeant lit the fuse. They all stood back to watch the missile blast out into the air and rise over the waves towards its target. There was a heavy sigh when it fell short, and the ship sailed on.

Still determined, the men used double the amount of powder to give more distance to the next ball, but before they could light the fuse, Ranald shouted and pointed to another ship entering the narrows. Working as one, the men realigned the cannon before taking very careful aim and lighting the fuse again. The ball skimmed over the water, taking what seemed like an age, before it dropped and hit the second target with a slight crackling sound. Disappointed, Dadda and Ranald could see no damage and turned away. The gunners were hastening to prime more gunpowder and get the last ball into the cannon. Dadda and Ranald put their fingers in their ears as they watched the smoking fuse burn down to the powder. All was quiet for a moment, then, finally, the gun roared.

The range looked good and the ball hit the vessel near its waterline, but to everyone's disappointment, the ship hardly faltered. Disappointed, they watched it following the other, seemingly without harm. Unperturbed, it sailed on through the narrows towards the open water beyond.

'Oh Dadda! I thought we had them.'

'Yes, Ranald. Me too. It's a pity, but we must be on our way.'

Roderick and the gunners too were disappointed as they packed up the gunpowder and readied the cannon for the long trek. After a final look at the ship, they turned their eyes northwards and set off along the mighty Great Glen towards Inverness.

Only gentle Ranald stayed to watch and it was his excited yell which made them all look back. The vessel was nearly out of sight, but they could see it was obviously listing badly, slowly sinking into Corran's churning waters. The men raised a cheer.

'Ah, well done!' said the gunnery sergeant. 'That is a good note to end on, but we'd better get a move on or the enemy will cut us off.'

They had no idea who was on board the ship they had just sunk.

CHAPTER 22

IT WAS THE FOLLOWING MORNING when a straggle of gunners heading north towards Inverness passed The Weaver's house. With cheery nods to the others, Dadda and Ranald turned their horses up the lane to make a quick visit with their sister Kate, The Weaver's wife. Roderick stayed with the other men.

After a few minutes, when young Donuill Dhu, who normally acted as a keen lookout, didn't come to challenge them, they knew something was wrong.

'Ranald, something is not right here. Be careful.'

Each brother took his knife from his stocking, fearing the worst. With a soft push, Dadda opened the front door, speaking aloud, 'God Bless all here.'

There was no response. All was dark, cold and empty, and the door through to the back room was shut. Dadda slowly unlatched the inner door. Once their eyes were adjusted to the darkness, they could see Kate curled up on the bed with five year-old Sandra clasped in her arms. The Weaver, dead and covered in blood, lay in a heap on the ground.

'Ranald, see if you can find some cloth to cover The Weaver, and get a fire going in the big room.'

He sat beside his shivering sister and silent niece, holding them close, and rocking to and fro with tears and gasps. He was too shocked to burden his sister with questions now, but soon Kate began to tell him what had happened.

It was a tragic tale. The previous afternoon, some of the Campbells from Inverawe had come up the road on their way to Inverness. Knowing that The Weaver Cameron was a Jacobite, one of the men slashed his way into the house and slew him without a word spoken, but ignored Kate and the child, leaving them in shock.

While she sobbed with tears running down her cheeks telling him the events, Dadda spoke no words, just listened. He could see that as she relayed the story to him she seemed to awake from the horror of what had occurred. She became quiet again so he felt he might leave them huddled together in their sorrow while he looked for something to ease their grief. When he returned, both mother and daughter were still sobbing together. He made them sup the whisky mixed with some curdled milk he'd found.

He went back into the big room and found Ranald arranging kindling and twigs on the hearth.

'I'll look after the fire. You go and find a spade.'

A few minutes later, his brother ran back in holding a spade saying, 'Donald the Bull is lying dead in the byre. Donuill Dhu is covered in blood as well and he is kneeling beside his uncle trying to shake him awake.'

A stunned Dadda stood up and ran to see for himself. When he entered the byre, he saw the Bull lying stretched out on the earth beside The Weaver's horse, while Donuill Dhu, bleeding from a wound to his arm, knelt, rocking back and forth and mumbling as he tried to rouse his uncle's bloody corpse.

'Come, laddie,' said Dadda, taking hold of the boy's arm. 'We must bring him into the house. Help me.'

Obediently, Donuill Dhu stood and helped Dadda as he hoisted The Bull onto his broad shoulders. As they headed for the house, the boy held one of the dead man's hands, until the burden was laid beside the table on the earthen floor of the big room.

Dadda sat Donuill Dhu down by the fire and brought him a bowl of the whisky and milk. While the boy mumbled and supped, watching over his uncle, Dadda went looking for more linen cloth. He soon found it among The Weaver's stock and as he ripped it into strips, he spoke quietly to calm the boy, then bound his bleeding arm.

Kate now felt safe to leave the back room. Clutching Sandra, she came to sit close to the new fire. She noticed The Bull lying dead on the floor, and then saw his nephew by the fire.

'Donuill Dhu,' she blurted out. 'You're alive.' With that she rushed over and knelt to embrace him. Dadda was still bandaging his arm.

'He'll be all right, Kate. He's a strong boy.'

'What are we going to do?'

'First, we have to take care of our dead.'

Kate began to sob again. The family of mourners were now tearfully all silent. Dadda tended the fire and then he brought Ranald outside.

He pointed across the grass to some trees. 'Ranald, take the spade and start digging two graves over there under those rowan trees. We'd better get it done sooner rather than later.'

'We can't stay here. We have to join the others at Inverness.'

'I know,' said Dadda. 'But first we must give them both a decent burial. Then we can be on our way.'

They returned to the house. Dadda cleared the table and with a nod to Ranald they went into the back room and brought The Weaver's body through and laid him on the table.

This somehow brought Kate to life. She too rose and went to the back room, and returned with the bloodstained sheet. After kissing The Weaver on each cold damp eyelid, she began to wrap her husband, whispering, 'Sleep well, my love.'

Conscious of Donuill Dhu's grief, Dadda went to the bedroom and found another sheet. When he brought it to The Bull, the boy took over the task of wrapping his uncle for the great journey to the hereafter.

Ranald found a prayer book on one of the shelves and when all were settled, he began to read aloud the prayers for the dead. Afterwards, Dadda asked Donuill Dhu to watch over his uncle's body, while he and Ranald, followed by Kate and Sandra, brought The Weaver to the newly dug graves.

The Bull was worthy of the same respect so Dadda and Ranald went back into the house and emerged with the corpse, followed by a solemn, silent Donuill Dhu. The mourners watched and prayed as both men were laid in their freshly dug graves, under the rowan trees.

They all knelt whilst Ranald again read more prayers to commend the souls of the two to Almighty God. Ranald and Dadda began to fill the graves as Kate and wee Sandra wept. Young Donuill Dhu sobbed incoherently and gathered some rowan branches from the graveside, while the last few spadesful of earth were patted down.

The solemn company returned to the house. 'Stoke up the fire, please, before it goes out.' Dadda gestured towards Donuill Dhu. He knew with a job to do, the lad would become a little more settled.

Kate was in no state to think of food, but when Dadda and Ranald found bannocks and soup and dried meat and laid them before her, habit caused her to find ale and whisky and bowls before she sat down and ate with them.

'The women and Donuill Dhu should be safe up in Glen Rowan, but it'll be a hard journey. One of us must go with them,' Dadda said to Ranald.

'You go, I'll head for Inverness, and catch up with Roderick and the others. I'm sure I will meet up with more clansmen on the way there,' said Ranald.

'I don't want to see you going,' Dadda reluctantly agreed, 'but we have no choice.'

It would be an hour or more before the sun began to fall behind the mountain, time enough to get ready to start the journey up to the safety of Glen Rowan. In the byre, Dadda and Donuill Dhu hitched The Weaver's cart to his horse and brought it to the door of the house.

'We can only take a few belongings so gather what you want, Kate, and let's get going.'

Kate settled Sandra into a corner of the cart, with trinkets and her special blanket around her and a hide to keep off any rain. She then went back into the house to retrieve her own precious mementos: fiddle, letters, jewellery, The Weaver's money from several secret places, and lastly his bagpipes.

Meanwhile, Dadda and Donuill Dhu were loading the cart with food they found in the store. They made sure that everyone had warm clothing.

Donuill Dhu got on Dadda's horse, now hitched at the back of the cart, and sat silently waving a couple of the rowan branches he'd taken from the grave. Soon they were one their way to the relative safety of Glen Rowan.

CHAPTER 23

IT WAS EARLY NEXT MORNING when Anghie ran up the path to the croft. 'Some people are coming, Sarah. They're still a bit far away, but from here, it looks like Dadda driving a cart, and someone on a horse behind them.'

'Oh dear,' said Sarah. 'Only locals come up here these days. It's probably them, but we'd better be careful until we know. Warn Jimmy and the girls to keep out of sight and be ready to run up to the still.'

Soon, to their relief, Sarah and Anghie could see that it was actually Dadda. They both rushed to help the travellers. It was a sorry sight they met. Kate and wee Sandra were silent, huddled together under some hides in a corner of the laden cart.

Sarah, realising it was young Donuill Dhu on the horse behind the cart, went to assist the tired and disoriented young rider to dismount, while Dadda helped the others into the house. With a nod to Sarah he said, 'Come and help me unharness the horse and get him into the byre with some fresh hay.'

While outside, Dadda told Sarah what they'd found at The Weaver's house. She was horrified, and then asked, 'Where is Uncle Ranald?'

'He is gone to Inverness and I must go soon.'

'You can't, Dadda. I need you here.'

Dadda knew she was right, but he had to follow Ranald and join the others at Inverness.

'We won't be long, Sarah. We'll have Cumberland retreating back down to England in no time at all.'

'But Dadda, I really need you here.'

With that she lost all control of her emotions and broke down, sobbing like a little child.

Dadda threw his arms around her. 'Sarah, Sarah, what's wrong?'

Sarah had to tell him, so in a quiet voice she whispered, 'Dadda, I'm expecting a baby.'

Dadda was both shocked and delighted. Amidst all the death and violence there was new life about to be born, and he was going to be a grandfather.

'Sarah, that's wonderful news,' he said as he hugged her tightly with tears in his eyes. 'I am so proud of you. I must stay and help you. You will need me even more now with Kate and her family here. I am sure our clansmen can manage Cumberland without me, although I am a little worried about Ranald.'

'Thank you, Dadda!'

Back inside, Kate and young Sandra held each other close and Sarah didn't disturb their sorrow when she entered. She laid food in front of them with a bowl of ale and whisky. They were still in shock, but the food could all wait there until bleak sorrow eased a little and hunger came upon them.

Anghie, the twins and young Jimmy all gathered

inside now and began to make up straw bed spaces for everyone around the wall of the big room, and stoked up the fire again. Kate and Sandra were the first to settle themselves in a corner. Sarah tucked one of The Weaver's blankets around them, and left them to rest. This was not the time for questions. Donuill Dhu also lay himself down, drew his cowhide around him and, quietly muttering his prayers, fell into an afternoon slumber.

When the mourners awoke later, Sarah, Anghie and the youngsters brought soup, bannocks, dried meat, ale and whisky to the table and all sat down.

Sarah spoke. 'Hamish was here. He came up to the glen, bringing welcome food and other useful things from Lizzie. However, he also had some startling news from Lizzie about Ian Og and Alistair.'

'Ian Og and Alistair? What did she say?' asked Dadda.

'Lizzie was visiting David at the fort a few days ago, and when she was leaving, Alistair and Ian Og were brought in as prisoners from the Cow Hill. She'd tucked herself into the shadows to watch, and saw Torquil MacLeod speaking to an officer who took immediate charge of the two, and marched them straight down the pier towards a couple of ships taking prisoners to work on the plantations overseas.'

'Is she sure it was Ian Og and Alistair?' Dadda was anxious.

'Yes she was positive, she knows them both well.'

'At least we know they are both still alive, but they're on their way to the Americas and we may never see them again.' Dadda was despondent and looked dejected.

'We will never see Ian Og again!' wailed Anghie,

as the little ones and all present looked stunned on hearing this news.

'How can we be sure?' Dadda asked. 'There must be some mistake.'

'No, it's true.' Sarah said. 'Hamish went to the fort to try and get more news. The soldiers knew him and were happy to chat. They had a record of some prisoners brought in the previous day; local drunks and some clansmen from the Craigs. Certainly nothing about any other captives prior to the plantation frigates casting off that afternoon. Just to make sure, Hamish also checked that there had been no firing squad or hangings within the fort that night. Hamish said that his mother had seen a subaltern take Alistair and Ian Og towards the ships bound for the American plantations, and was fairly sure that they were put on board the last ship to sail.'

Sarah gave a sigh and continued, 'I was so very relieved to know both of them had escaped execution. At the very least, the American plantations are better than a hanging.'

'Where is Lizzie now? Most of the soldiers from Fort William are heading to Inverness to join up with Cumberland's forces,' said Dadda.

'Yes they are, and Lizzie is with her man. Hamish and Lizzie caught up with them on General Wade's road. Hamish told me that he was happy to say that his mother had at last found herself a decent man who, like herself, was originally from Dornoch. He left his home many years ago and although he is now in enemy forces, he has fallen for Lizzie as she has for him. The war isn't going to last forever.'

As Sarah was speaking, Dadda seemed uncomfortable, and was becoming more and more subdued as he considered all that was being said.

'I am now concerned about Hamish. His parting words were that once he'd taken his mother to join David, he would return to the glen. I haven't seen him since then. Where is Uncle Ranald?'

'He's gone to Inverness, to join the others. Everyone is going to Inverness.'

'Oh, I'm sorry,' Sarah said. 'I've been going on, haven't I, and I haven't asked what you and Uncle Ranald had been doing. What was Corran like? It was good that you were able to call in to Auntie Kate and get the three of them up here, after what happened to The Weaver and The Bull. They'll all be better off away from that Linnhe Road.'

With a deep sigh, Dadda spoke. 'Oh, Sarah. I knew I brought bad news about The Weaver, but I thought I had good news about our activities at the Corran.'

'We could do with some good news,' interjected Sarah.

'You should have seen us. We were with the gunners and during the day we had a fair bit of success, but of course when word came that Cumberland and the Hanoverian army was heading up from Aberdeen, all the rest of the Jacobite artillery was called up to Inverness.' Dadda sighed. 'Night was falling and it was too late for us to set off so we were preparing the guns for the next day's trip to Inverness, when Ranald spotted two ships. Two large ships!'

He took a sup from his cup. 'They were the last ships and they were heading towards the narrows, and we were supposed to be on our way to Inverness. Who could resist it, Sarah? We had only three cannonballs left. The forge and the smith were already gone, so these were the last we had. It was too good a chance to miss.'

'What happened?' Sarah asked, as all of them listened intently.

'We stopped, loaded the cannon and took a chance. It was really disappointing when the first fell short of the target, and although we used more gunpowder, the second had not enough strength either. Then ... the last one ... the very last one ... it went straight and hit the second ship. We watched as the ship tilted, and sank slowly into the water. It was a wonderful moment.'

'Hurrah!' screeched Anghie suddenly.

Dadda continued. 'Oh Sarah, Sarah ... Ian Og ... Ian Og ... my son.... and Alistair.' He wiped his tears away. 'What if Ian Og and Alistair were on that ship? We had NO idea.' He laid his forehead down upon the table ... and was silent.

In shock, Sarah laid her head against Anghie's shoulder and let her tears flow. 'Dadda, you are saying they're dead?' She mumbled as the meaning of her own words sank in.

'They were too far out from the shore amid the raging torrents. Everyone knows the waters are treacherous there. The ship and all on board were lost for sure,' said Dadda.

'But we don't know they were on that ship.' Sarah refused to accept that they might have been.

A long silence followed as each digested the news. Sarah was the first to speak. 'We have to be strong. That's what Alistair and Ian Og would want us to do, but I don't feel strong.'

Dadda said, 'You're right, Sarah, and I don't feel strong either. However, we have to accept the situation. All we can do is hope that they did not die.'

Anghie stood up trying to find something positive to say. 'Let us toast the coming of the true sovereign

Prince Charles, rightful heir to King James.'

Reluctantly, they all raised their bowls to toast but their hearts were not in it. Sarah, trying to blink away her tears, went and fetched another flagon of Angus's best whisky from his secret store. As the evening wore on there was little chat as everyone got on with their chores.

Next morning, it was a very hungover company which gathered around the big table. Sarah was wondering whether her headache was the result of a surfeit of tears or whisky or both. She needed space to think. Kate had already risen and collected a couple of bannocks for Sandra and herself, before returning to her bed space where Sandra still lay.

Several times Dadda rose and put his arms firmly around Sarah to comfort her. 'Oh, dearest Sarah. We were there. We didn't know.'

Each time, Sarah said, 'Aww, Dadda ...' and let her head fall again into her hands, repeating, 'I can't believe it.'

While those in the house began to rise, Sarah made sure that there was fresh food for the table. Fresh water from the well lay at the back door and, and with shaky steps, she brought a flagon and filled it, then returned and put it on the table. She filled her own bowl and speedily drank the water down before leaving the croft.

Sarah went to the little graveyard where her mother and Grannie Morag were buried. She always felt a certain calm come over her there. The baby kicked within her belly as if to say 'I'm still here', as she thought about all that had happened.

After a while, she felt she wasn't alone somehow. She became refreshed and much more whole. She could feel a sense of Grannie Morag frantically fluttering round her, trying to tell her something. As she broke off several new shoots from the rowan trees around her, she heard someone whisper. 'They're safe, Sarah.' She quickly spun around but there was no one there.

'Grannie Morag!' she called out, but there was no reply. She waited for several minutes as she replayed in her mind what she had just heard.

Finally, she called out again. 'Thank you, Grannie Morag.'

She ran all the way back to the croft and sat down beside Dadda. 'They are safe!' she exclaimed. 'I know they're safe. Grannie Morag sent me a message.'

'Ah, Sarah.' He shook his head. 'We saw, we watched. They're gone.'

'No, Dadda,' Sarah spoke firmly. 'They are safe.'

'They are DEAD, Sarah.'

'NO, Dadda ... stop ... clear your mind ... and feel ... feel.' After a moment she asked, 'what can you feel, Dadda?'

'Oh, Sarah.' Again he stretched his arms out to his daughter. 'We saw it. We all saw it. I am sorry. It's true.'

'NO.' This time it was a much quieter Sarah who made the statement. She sat down.

'NO.' She repeated. 'When I was at the graveyard under the rowans, I could FEEL that they live. Deep in my heart, I know they're still here. Grannie Morag told me. I am sure of it.'

Dadda paused. There was no way to contradict his determined daughter. He took a deep breath. With eyes closed he firmly clasped Sarah's hand ... and at that moment he felt a warmth envelop his whole body, casting out the sadness within him.

He shouted, 'Yes, Yes! It's true. I can't believe it, but I can feel it, I can feel it too.'

'What can you feel, Dadda?'

'They're alive,' he said. 'I know they're alive.' Dadda rubbed his chin and said, 'It could be a long time before they can be seen in this area.'

'And I remember something else,' Sarah said.

'It's making sense now. Hamish told me that there were two horses missing from the forge when he went back there, and there was a note saying that the horses would be returned. He thought somebody going to Inverness took them. It meant nothing to me, but it must have been Alistair and Ian Og. Who else would leave a note?'

Then Dadda said, 'That's a sign, Sarah, they left a sign for us. We must not tell anyone that they are alive. We don't want soldiers looking for them.'

'We will just have to wait,' Sarah said. 'But one day they will return.'

Also by Anne L. MacDonell

GLEN ROWAN

Inspired by family stories passed down through the generations, author Anne L. MacDonell weaves an unforgettable tale of drama and intrigue, battles and betrayal.

Set in the rugged Scottish Highlands in 1740, thirteen-year-old Sarah and her brother Ian Og set out from their Glen Rowan home on what should be a special trip to town. While their uncle Angus goes about his business selling whisky, the MacDonell children go off to explore Maryburgh. When the pair witness two soldiers from Fort William thrashing a boy not much older than themselves, they rush to his aid. Alistair Glic, a fisherman, helps them escape but he is more than he appears at first. He is, in fact, in the service of Bonnie Prince Charlie and the Jacobite army. Before long, they all find themselves entangled in the events that shaped Scotland's history.

Printed in Great Britain
by Amazon

32086300R00128